Snowed In with the Cowboy

 Horseshoe Home Ranch

LIZ ISAACSON

ISBN-13: 978-1-63876-239-3

Cast thy burden upon the Lord, and he shall sustain
thee: he shall never suffer the righteous to be moved."

— PSALMS 55:22

CHAPTER 1

The announcer's voice reverberated through Sterling Maughan's head, bringing him away from the edge of unconsciousness and back to the X-Games blaring from the TV.

He knew that voice. Hated that voice, especially after it had broken up with him on live, national television.

He fumbled for the remote so he could change the channel, the pain in his leg amping up to a sharp ache. One glance at the clock on the Blu-ray player told him he'd missed his last dosage of painkillers by an hour.

Sterling didn't care. When the nurse came, she'd force-feed it to him. He hit a button and that traitorous, cheating female voice changed into the theme song for a cooking show. He lowered the volume and dropped the remote. It made a weird clunking sound as it hit last night's pizza box. Or maybe last week's pizza box. Sterling had stopped cleaning up after his first night at the cabin, eight days ago.

Sleep eluded him for a few minutes as he listened to the evening wind batter the windows. At least it wasn't the neighbors—the closest ones up here in Gold Valley's exclusive cabin community were at least a hundred yards away.

Not that Sterling had been admiring the lush pine forest and miles of trails surrounding his family's cabin. He hadn't moved from the couch in the basement for more than the necessities for days. His eyes drifted closed and he sank into the darkness that had consumed his mind so readily since the accident.

A thump from the second floor jolted him awake. His heart pounded as his mind frantically searched for an explanation to the sound. The wind had died, but it could've been an animal. Could've been a raccoon or a rat.

A scrape echoed through the ceiling, like someone—*not* a raccoon or a rat—had slid a chair across the floor. Sterling sat up, fully awake now.

Because someone was in the house.

He calmed his breathing and swallowed his pulse back to its proper spot in his chest. His police training required him to be alert, focused, and calm in stressful situations. True, he hadn't been active in his unit since last fall, when he'd started the professional snowboarding circuit. But once a cop, always a cop.

He stood, careful to put minimal weight on his still-healing knee. The cast had come off last week, but he still wore a full leg brace, which made walking difficult. And climbing stairs? Sterling hadn't done it in weeks.

His back creaked with his first step, and his left foot felt numb because of the reduced circulation from the brace. A pain behind his right eye balanced both sides of his body with aches he couldn't erase with a couple of pills.

Another noise—*bump, ba-bump*—from the second floor urged him toward the stairs, where he lifted his injured leg first. One down, fifteen to go.

For the first time, he cursed the size of the cabin. Seven thousand square feet, spanning three floors. Two kitchens, one on the main level where the noise came from, one in the basement where he was living. Ten bathrooms. Eight bedrooms. A game room, a library, and two living rooms.

His father had done very well in the real estate business, as his mother liked to point out to Sterling about every third month. He'd never been a conformist, and it showed as all five of his older brothers had gone on to law school at William & Mary, or medical school at Johns Hopkins, or banking and finance at Stanford.

Sterling had graduated in the middle of his class from the Police Academy in Salt Lake City.

Still, he steadily climbed the stairs, two feet planted before lifting that blasted left leg. His mind wandered through a list of who could possibly be at the cabin. His parents had gone to Madagascar for a university internship in January and certainly wouldn't return only three months into the eight-month program.

His brothers all had a key to the cabin, but everyone but Rex lived in other states. Rex lived in Missoula, an hour and a half away, running their father's real estate brokering firm, and he hadn't mentioned coming up to the cabin.

Sterling's fingers fisted, almost hoping for a fight. At least he knew the police officer in him hadn't been snuffed out. He didn't know if he'd be able to return to the force, what with his injuries and all, but he felt confident in his abilities to incapacitate—

—A curvy woman.

Sterling stalled at the top of the stairs and stared at the dark-skinned, dark-haired woman standing in the kitchen, leaning over something he couldn't see. She wore a tight pair of jeans and a long-sleeved shirt—not exactly burglary clothing.

Women can be killers too, he thought just before the loudest music he'd ever heard blasted through the house.

The woman shook her booty to the music as she pulled on a pair of yellow rubber gloves. Sterling stared, wondering if she'd put on the rap to cover the sound of his screams and the gloves to prevent the possibility of leaving fingerprints. He couldn't decide if he should dial 911 or laugh at her terrible dance moves.

A smile formed on his face—possibly the first since his fall eleven weeks ago. He suddenly became aware that he hadn't showered or shaved in many days, and fought the urge to rush downstairs and attend to his personal hygiene needs.

As he scrubbed his fingers along his scruffy beard, the woman spun around, her eyes half open. Open enough to catch on his though, and she stopped short. Her gloved hand came to her mouth—*gross,* Sterling thought—and her chocolaty eyes widened.

He lifted his hand in greeting, his smile reducing itself by half. She spun and fumbled at the source of the hip-hop beat, finally silencing it. She placed one hand over her heart as her chest rose and fell, rose and fell. "You scared me."

Sterling leaned against the wall to give some relief to his aching leg, but otherwise held his position. "What's up?"

"Nothing." The woman gestured to a bucket of cleaning supplies at her feet. "I'm here to clean the cabin." She glanced around like someone would appear to corroborate her story. "I didn't know anyone would be here."

Sterling's gaze swept the counter behind her, focusing on several bags of groceries. "Are you staying?"

"Yes." She followed his gaze to the fruit and bread. "I'm bringing my girls up here tonight."

"Girls?" Confusion clouded Sterling's mind, his words. "What girls?"

"I work at the teen rehabilitation center at the base of the mountain," she explained. "You know, Silver Creek, the one with the horses?"

Sterling had been coming to his family's cabin his entire life. He'd never heard of a teen rehabilitation center. "No, I have no idea about Silver Creek or the horses."

"Oh, well, I work there." The woman spoke with her hands, and Sterling worried about the germs spewing from those gloves, though they were probably cleaner than he was. She seemed to realize how ridiculous she looked with those toilet gloves on, because she stripped them off as a dark red stained her cheeks.

"It's a rehabilitation program for teens with addictions,"

she continued. "They live on-site for ninety days, and part of their therapy is to learn to work with horses as they overcome their problems. I'm a counselor." She took a deep breath, probably because she hadn't done so once since she started talking.

Sterling cocked one eyebrow at the speed with which she delivered her spiel. "And?"

"And I clean your family's cabin. I've been doing it for a few years."

"And you bring your girls up here?"

"When they reach the halfway point of their stay, they get to go on an outing if they've followed the rules and stayed clean. Your mom has given me permission to bring them to Six Sons. We'll be here for three days."

Oh, no they wouldn't. Sterling had some very important recovering to do. Alone. No teen addicts. No beautiful, exotic camp counselors. Just pizza and cooking shows and sleeping while the drugs kept the pain at bay.

"You're Sterling Maughan," the woman said.

Sterling felt the weight of her proclamation, spoken in a tone of awe and reverence like he was worthy of such things. "Yeah."

She blinked a couple of times, and Sterling could practically hear the words she wanted to say before she said them. *Terrible about what that Amber Lyons did to you. And on national TV too.*

He braced himself as she opened her mouth. "I'm Norah Watson." Her eyes scanned his height, coming back to his face a moment later. "I'm sorry about your fall. Will you ever snowboard again?"

Ah, wasn't that the question of the year? Sterling didn't know the answer, so he lifted one shoulder in a half-shrug. Emotion surged up his throat, along with the feel of the wind against his face, the smell of a fresh snowfall, where it stuck no matter how hard he tried to swallow it back.

"I've seen you race," she said. "You were like liquid on the mountain. So smooth."

"Thanks," he managed to croak. He actually would've preferred she gave him her condolences about his ex-girl-friend. He'd at least be able to find another date someday. But snowboarding had always come before women, and he couldn't articulate yet how much he'd lost when he'd lost snowboarding.

"You can't stay here," he said, his rough voice matching the shredded edges in his chest.

Panic crossed her face, troubling her lips and causing a twitch in her fingers. "But I have to. The girls have been working so hard for this outing."

Unrest swirled in his gut. "*I'm* staying here for a while." How long, he didn't know. He didn't have anything else to do, and nowhere else to go, and no one to see.

Norah began unpacking the groceries. "How about we strike a deal?"

"A deal?" Sterling folded his arms and watched her work.

"You're obviously living downstairs." She tossed him a look over her shoulder that said, *Right?*

He didn't indicate an answer either way, just waited for her to continue.

"This place is three levels. We always stay upstairs in the bunk bed room." She glanced to the ceiling like she could see the bunk beds from here. "I have eight girls in my group, and you won't even know we're here. We'll stay on the top two levels. There's a kitchen here, and one downstairs for you." She gave him another up-down glance. "You're obviously not going to be traipsing around the property, and we'll be gone before you even know we're here."

He doubted it. He'd heard her, and he'd been half-asleep. What would eight teenage girls sound like?

Chickens, he thought. *Or elephants.*

"I have to turn in a strict itinerary for these outings." She reached for a binder on the counter. "You can see our schedule if you want. We'll be gone cross-country skiing most of the morning tomorrow, and I only let them go down to the game room once, on Saturday evening, and we'll be back in bed by ten both nights. I promise."

She lifted a paper toward him, but Sterling waved it away. Though the game room took up considerable space in the basement, where he was living, he hadn't used it since he'd arrived, and he wasn't planning to. He barely used the kitchen in the basement, opting to pick up his cell phone and order, well, pizza.

"I don't want a bunch of girls here."

"But you won't even know we're here."

"I knew you were here." He gave her a pointed look.

"And I have my home health nurses coming twice a day. That can't be disrupted."

"Of course not. And I won't blast any rap music." She crossed her heart. "Only Mozart. Soothing. I promise." Her lips tugged upward, and something slipped in Sterling's resolve.

"I don't know…the doctor said I need a lot of rest." He glanced out the windows located above the spiral staircase that led downstairs. "My mom didn't say anything about this when I told her I was coming here."

Norah smiled like she'd won. "Well, I'll call Nancy right now and ask her."

When she mentioned his mom, Sterling felt the victory blow land against his lungs. The last thing he wanted was to talk to her, especially after their last conversation.

"Don't do that," he said. "I guess I can put up with you for three days."

———

Norah put away the rest of the groceries under the misses-nothing eye of Sterling Maughan. *The* Sterling Maughan. The one who'd won gold at the last Olympics and had been set to sweep every event in this winter's X-Games.

Of course, that was before the Break-Up to End All Break-Ups, and then the devastating fall that had broken his left femur and shattered part of his pelvis.

He looked good for such an injury, standing there glowering at her, wearing a T-shirt that pulled across his broad shoulders, a loose pair of gym shorts, and the bulkiest leg brace she'd ever seen. At least he could stand, and he certainly hadn't lost his brooding good looks in the accident. Norah had seen enough interviews to know.

"Do you need help getting down the stairs?" She didn't turn to look at him as she asked. Someone with as many muscles as Sterling could snap her in half with his bare hands. He didn't look as though he'd lost anything in the bicep department since his accident.

His dark eyes didn't dance the way they had on the medal podium, though. And while she'd seen him in countless family photos—always alone, surrounded by his five brothers and their wives and families—she hadn't realized how dark his hair was. The colors on her old TV were obviously lacking.

"I could use some help, yes."

His words surprised her, but she crossed through the kitchen and stepped down the two stairs to the living room. This particular staircase that led to the basement spiraled, and she knew from experience that going down was harder than going up. Especially because the last three stairs were very steep and quite uneven.

"I'll go first," she said. "You can brace your weight on my shoulders." She moved down a few steps and stopped. The heat of his hands on her shoulders sent a shiver through her she hoped he didn't notice.

Giddiness swept through her. Her half-brother would

never believe she'd met Sterling Maughan, the professional athlete that was made from all gold for the people in Gold Valley. As they moved painstakingly down the steps, Norah toyed with the idea of asking him for a picture. Would she come off as a gushing fan? A lunatic? Some flirty girl? Utterly insensitive?

When they reached the bottom floor, Norah gasped at the sight of the living room. A nest—a real, live, human-sized nest!—on the couch showed where Sterling had obviously been living. Soda cans, pizza boxes, paper wrappers, straws, and clothes littered the floor in a six-foot radius from the nest.

"How long have you been here?" she asked, taking in the unlit fireplace, the TV glowing with instructions on how to grill ribs above the mantle. He obviously hadn't used any of the three bedrooms down here. The door to the closest bathroom stood open, but all the blinds on the wall of windows that would normally show a deck and breathtaking winter scenery had been tightly shut.

"Since last week." Sterling hobbled into the kitchen—much smaller than the one on the main floor, but certainly sufficient for this bachelor sixth son.

She followed him, freezing as he downed a handful of pills. Just the sound the caplets made against the plastic bottle conjured old hurts and images she'd rather forget. She forced her feet to move and reached under the sink for a garbage bag. Fluffing it open, she began to fill it with a week's worth of fast food waste.

"You don't have to do that," Sterling said.

"It's my job." Norah winced as she caught a whiff of Sterling's socks. "Your mom pays me to do this."

Sterling made a grab for a pair of discarded board shorts, and Norah pulled back. "I don't need you to do my laundry."

"I don't do laundry."

"Great."

"But I'm killer at picking up trash." She gave him a wide berth as she moved around the couch and reached for the pizza box. The remote fell off, and she put it on the coffee table.

"I can do it." But Sterling sank back into his nest and lifted his injured leg with his hands. He groaned as he placed it on the stack of pillows he'd laid out on the coffee table.

A flash of what life would be like if Norah had a lot of money stole through her head. Yes, the sports news feeds had been full of *Poor Sterling Maughan. His career is over just as it was picking up momentum. And too bad about his girlfriend being such a cheater....*

But "poor Sterling Maughan" was anything but poor. He wasn't working two jobs and going to school at night just to pay the electric bill and put food on the table and make sure his mama had the medicine she needed.

Norah tasted the bitterness of her situation on the back of her tongue, and it was too familiar. She hated feeling this way, and yet she couldn't push down the negative vibes.

She stuck a smile on her face as she tied the now-full

trash bag. "Hey, can I ask a huge favor? My half-brother is a big fan of yours. Could I get a picture with you?"

Sterling looked up, his eyes half glazed from the pills. Strong jealousy Norah hadn't felt in a while surged through her. She managed to push it away.

"Sure, I guess." The disinterest in his voice didn't fall on deaf ears, but Norah whipped her phone from her back pocket anyway. She wanted to spray an entire can of disinfectant on his nest before she touched it, but she flopped down on the blanket at his side like it was a throne fit for a queen. A puff of foul-smelling air surrounded them, but Norah contained the cringe.

"Okay, smile." She focused on the two of them, but Sterling's smile looked more like a grimace. Maybe she'd jostled his leg too much. Something whispered inside her that it wasn't just his leg giving him trouble.

Norah snapped the picture and turned toward Sterling. Close enough for her breath to brush his cheek. He kept his mouth steadfastly shut, and if she had to guess, she should be happy she couldn't smell his breath.

As she watched him, she felt his sadness penetrate her defenses. Felt his helplessness. Her mother had always told her she had a compassionate heart and was able to sense someone in distress.

"I'm sorry," she whispered, unable to break eye contact with the damaged once-pro-snowboarder.

He blinked, shrugged, laid his head back, closed his eyes. "It happens."

Norah stood, haunted by the finality in his tone. *Help*

him, she prayed, unable to do much more than that for the man who wore his emotional turmoil so openly. As she went back upstairs to finish preparations for her girls, she promised herself she'd check in on Sterling over the next couple of days. Even though he had nurses coming, he seemed like he could use a friend.

CHAPTER 2

$\mathcal{N}$orah maneuvered down the mountain from Six Sons Cabin, careful to stay near the center of the road. March had been brutal in the weather department, and the merrily shining sun only lent light, not warmth. Certainly not enough heat to melt the snow and ice this high above sea level.

She checked the clock on the dashboard and eased up on the brakes. She needed to return to Silver Creek before two o'clock so she could take her girls to their weekly riding session. After that, they usually went to dinner in the cafeteria, but tonight, they'd load into a Silver Creek van and head up to the cabin. She was glad, because the cafeteria was currently under construction in preparation for a complete makeover.

Norah was planning a cookout and had quickly swept the snow off the second-level deck before leaving Sterling to his painkillers and cooking shows. The image of his sunken eyes pulled at her heart. On TV, he'd always been full of life and quick to pump his fist after a successful run. The man she'd met had become a shell of the one she'd seen on TV, a ghost of who she saw in the pictures scattered around the cabin.

You need to help him. The thought entered her mind unbidden, and Norah felt its power. Her fingers tightened on the wheel as she rounded the last bend in the road before it straightened out and dipped into the valley.

"How?" she asked herself. She had no idea how to deal with an injury like Sterling's, though she did understand why people smoked, or drank, or turned to cutting. Having experienced similar home conditions as the girls she worked with, she'd dealt with her share of problems and temptations.

The pull to escape her life just for an hour threaded through her. A single painkiller would give her those sixty minutes.

The constant emotional effort she had to expend to take care of her mama sometimes weighed Norah down to the point where she couldn't get out of bed until she psyched herself up.

Normal twenty-seven-year-olds didn't care for their half-brothers full time, play nursemaid to a woman who should be able to take care of herself, or mother eight troubled teens. As Norah turned a corner, she wanted the life that single women her age enjoyed. And with that yearning came a punch of guilt that hit her right in the lungs.

She pushed away the tide of bitter feelings. Her three

half-brothers depended on Norah for everything, and with their mama sick, Norah certainly couldn't add another invalid to her plate. And yet, she felt a strong attraction to Sterling that went beyond his celebrity status.

She parked in the staff lot and leapt from her car, determined to think about Sterling later. As she stopped by the administration office to turn in the girls' permission slips, she found Dr. Richards dictating a job notice to his secretary.

Norah listened as she flipped through the pages she already knew were in order. When Dr. Richards finished, Norah handed him the papers. "We're headed up to Six Sons tonight. We'll be back on Monday in time for dinner."

Dr. Richards didn't look at the permission paperwork. "Sounds good, Norah. I want you to pay particular attention to Genn while you're up there. She had a hard session this morning."

Norah nodded and swung her chin toward the secretary. "You need a new counselor?"

Dr. Richards handed the paperwork to his secretary and stepped into his office, a sigh filled with exhaustion escaping his lips. "Yes, Will quit today. He's staying on until the end of this cycle." He settled at his desk and pulled a file toward him. "I know you'd take on another group, but I need a male."

"I might know someone." Norah spoke before she could think. Or maybe Sterling had never really left her mind.

"Oh?" Dr. Richards glanced up and held her gaze. "Who? What experience does he have?"

"Well, he probably doesn't have any." Norah twisted her fingers around themselves. Why had she spoken?

"Is he over twenty-five?"

"Yes." Norah had seen Sterling snowboard countless times, had watched a couple of interviews on ESPN, and knew he was twenty-six.

"He's not employed?"

Norah thought of Sterling's nest, the greasy texture of his hair, the length of that beard, the smell of his dirty socks. "He…he used to be a cop. But he got hurt."

Dr. Richards perked up. "A cop? Maybe he could work with our at-risk group."

The at-risk boys that came to Silver Creek often had violent histories, usually involving weapons rather than drugs.

"Maybe," Norah said.

"Get an application from Shelly," Dr. Richards said. "See if he wants to apply."

Norah said good-bye and stepped into the outer office to get an application for Sterling. With the single sheet of paper in her hand, she felt like she had something concrete to do for him.

Ten minutes later, she stood at the end of the hall on the second floor of the girls' building. "Team Silver Bow!" she called. The four doors nearest her opened within a few seconds of each other and her eight girls entered the hall.

They each wore the required horseback attire: long pants, long-sleeved shirts, and boots. They carried coats and hats and gloves. Norah smiled at each girl, noticing that

Genn's eyes stayed on the floor, and her roommate, Hailey, seemed to have been crying.

Though her motherly instincts kicked in, Norah kept quiet. It wasn't her job to provide therapy. She was there to facilitate their schedules, get them to meals on time, establish the rules, and be a listening ear should the girls choose to tell her something. Nothing the girls told her was private, and Norah hated that, but it kept her out of difficult situations.

"You ready to ride?" she asked.

Varying responses came from the girls, ranging from mild interest to sarcasm to genuine enthusiasm. Norah stepped to the head of the line and led them downstairs and around the building. As they entered the March wind, Norah sucked in a breath and prayed for an early spring.

"Just think, ladies," she said over her shoulder. "In just a couple of hours, we'll be sitting by a huge fireplace, sipping hot chocolate."

Natalie, a bubbly fourteen-year-old, cheered from behind her. "Can I ride Kimchi today?"

"You ride who you're given," Norah said. "But I'll try to line you up with her."

The girls entered the barn, where Silver Creek's wrangler had eight horses already in stalls. He came out of the tack room, saw the girls, and adjusted his white cowboy hat. "Afternoon, ladies."

One of the girls giggled, and Norah sent a glare down the line. The strict non-fraternizing rules sometimes wore on the girls, especially the flirtier ones. They hadn't seen or spoken to a boy in six weeks, besides Dr. Richards and Owen, the horseman now smiling down on them in all his Montana cowboy glory.

He pointed to the horses behind him. "We got a new gelding this mornin'. His name's Pompeii. Who wants to ride 'im first?" Owen's gaze swept the girls, his keen eyes searching for something Norah didn't understand.

"Genn?" Owen asked, leaving Norah to wonder if Owen could read more than horses.

"Sure." Genn stepped over to the unfamiliar dark horse with a black mane and tail.

"Nat," Norah hissed. "Trade places with Felicia."

The two girls switched, and Natalie got assigned to Kimchi, the brown and white paint horse she preferred. Norah stayed in the barn as Owen reminded the girls how to mount the horse and hold the reins. Her chest filled with love as Genn leaned over and patted Pompeii's neck, a smile pulling at the corner of her mouth. Norah had experienced many "hard sessions" during her time at Silver Creek, and as much as she didn't want to, she saw herself in Genn. A good girl, without the resources or support to do much with her life.

But in the six weeks since Genn arrived, Norah had seen strides in her she hadn't experienced herself. Genn's parents had started coming to the group counseling sessions, something Mama had never done for Norah.

Warmth expanded in Norah's chest. Genn would make it. She'd do something great with her life, not be confined to Gold Valley and her childhood home the way Norah was.

Norah wanted nothing but success and happiness for the girl, for all her girls.

For Sterling too, she thought, startled by how easily the man had wormed his way into her mind. She'd spent maybe fifteen minutes with him—which was fifteen more minutes than she'd spent with someone of the opposite sex in quite a long time.

That's why, she told herself as she waited for the girls to return from their ride. Since she still lived at home with her three younger half-brothers—and her sick mama—Norah didn't have time to go on many dates, what with two jobs and a night class. And she wasn't all that interested in growing close to a man only to watch him leave when things got hard.

She'd seen that too many times in Mama's life. Their front door seemed to rotate with men. But when the bills piled too high, or the baby cried too loud, or Mama got too demanding, those men left.

Norah had never left. She couldn't. Especially not now with Mama's lung disease so advanced and so debilitating. The swell of resentment reared again, nearly choking her.

Her phone rang, and she swiped open the call from her half-brother, Javier. "What's up?"

"Hey, Norah. Mama said it's your girls' weekend, but I want to go to the movies with Sarah and Mateo."

Norah smiled at the rush in Javier's voice and waited while he presented his case.

"So I went and got a movie for Alex and Erik, and they're

set with popcorn and hot chocolate. I just wanted to run it by you, make sure it's okay."

A pinch behind Norah's eyes reminded her that she wasn't the only one paying the price for Mama's illnesses. "Do you have enough money for the movies?"

"Yeah. Anthony paid me this morning." Javier worked for the Mexican grocer as much as possible, but Norah could never take his money, even if she sometimes needed it. A senior in high school, Javier would have to make his own ends meet soon enough.

"Okay. Who's driving?"

"Mateo."

Norah nodded though Javier couldn't see her. Sarah had slid into a snow bank last winter, and Norah felt safer with Mateo driving. "Sounds like you've got it worked out."

"I do, Norah. Thanks."

She hung up, glad for her girls' weekend. She needed the time away from Mama's depression, her medication schedule, her pessimism. Sometimes Norah wondered if she babied her mother too much, but she wasn't sure how not to. She'd been forced to act as mother way before she should've, and a sticky film coated her mouth as she tried to swallow back the trapped feelings. They came every so often, and Norah couldn't help wondering if her mind was as messed up as Mama's.

To prove she wasn't a slave to her demons, Norah poured everything she had into taking care of her girls. At least with them, she could witness growth and change and healing—something she'd never see in her mama. Sadness filled her, and her soul ached for a solution to her mother's mental and physical challenges. She wanted to help, she just didn't know how.

Again, Sterling's handsome face filled her mind, and a smidgeon of annoyance sang through her.

———

Sterling heard the girls enter the cabin shortly after five o'clock. He'd just come out of the bathroom, where he'd showered and shaved for the first time in several days. It had been as hard as he'd anticipated, even with the shower bench that provided some relief for his leg. Simply getting the brace off had taken him five minutes.

Frustration flooded him as he considered the brace. He really didn't want to put it back on, but he felt the weakness in his leg without it. He didn't want his recovery to take longer than necessary, but reasoned that a few more minutes without the brace wouldn't set him back that much.

He picked up his phone—no messages, no calls—and almost slammed it back onto the kitchen counter. Before the accident, he hadn't been able to keep up with the number of people wanting to talk to him. Family and friends. Those who wanted to be friends. People who wanted an interview, or to talk about a sponsorship, or to film his practice session.

Gratitude filled him that no cameras or reporters had been at the practice session when he'd fallen. The last thing he needed was to watch that horror over and over again on the Internet.

"Sterling?" Norah's voice bounced down the steps. Her body followed a few seconds later, screeching to a halt when she found him leaning against the kitchen counter. Her eyes brightened, slid down the length of his body. When they returned to his again, he saw the same look he'd seen in other girls' eyes. Appreciation. Maybe something a bit warmer.

"You're up." Her voice sounded flirtier, and Sterling couldn't help the zing of satisfaction spiraling through him. He'd been desirable once. Even though his phone sat silent, here was a woman looking at him as if she liked what she saw. That had to count for something.

She grinned at him, and he found himself returning it, thinking maybe *she* could be his friend. "You shaved."

Sterling rubbed his hands along his jaw. "Yeah, it was time." His gaze lingered on her curly hair and sparkling eyes, his face heating when he realized *he* liked what he saw too.

"I'm making hamburgers and hot dogs for the girls." She hooked her thumb over her shoulder toward the stairs. "You want one?"

Sterling's stomach grumbled. "Sure."

"Which? Hamburger or hot dog?"

"Yes," Sterling said, and Norah laughed.

"Okay, both. It'll be a few minutes."

"Take your time." Sterling watched her head back up the stairs before he allowed himself to scan the living room. His clothes still lay scattered around and the room seemed too dark.

He limped over to the window and opened the blinds that faced north, but they let in very little light now that the sun had started to go down. Still, with the view of snow-covered pines and a dusky sky, new life entered his body.

He bent to pick up his clothes. After one trip to the laundry room, Sterling's leg throbbed in protest. He took the time to strap on the brace before he finished tidying up.

Norah returned with two plates filled with a hamburger, a hot dog, coleslaw, potato chips and baby carrots. Embarrassment flooded Sterling's cheeks. "Wow, you think I can eat all that?"

"I have three brothers," she said. "I *know* you can eat all that."

He chuckled as she set the plates on the kitchen counter. "And you even made sure I got vegetables." Sterling slid her a glance, hoping she'd hear the teasing note in his voice. "You make your girls eat all their vegetables?"

She stared at him with a blank face. "Absolutely. Carrots are the building blocks of nutrition for wayward girls."

Sterling settled onto a barstool as he laughed, glad when Norah joined in. "This might be the first meal I haven't eaten on the couch or in bed since my accident."

Norah leaned against the pillar next to the fridge. "Is the burger cooked okay?"

Sterling bit into it, immediately categorizing the meat as overcooked. Charred might be a better description. He forced himself to chew, chew, chew, and swallow. "Delicious." He picked up a bottle of water and downed half of it to get the dry beef to slide down his throat.

Norah seemed to swell under his compliment, and a kernel of interest popped inside Sterling. What kind of person was she? Why did she work with addicted teenagers? How did she come to be cleaning cabins in this exclusive gated community?

"So you don't have any sisters?" Sterling asked, skillfully avoiding taking another bite by engaging in conversation.

"Nope."

"Me either."

"I know," Norah said. "I've been dusting your pictures for years. You were a cute kid." Her smile infected him, and a layer of darkness lifted from his mind.

"Cute." He ate a few potato chips—surely Norah hadn't made those—wondering if anyone would ever find him worth more than *cute*. He could barely put weight on his leg, and the angry, red scars proved he still had a long road ahead of him.

"Anyway, I've got to get back to the girls. I just wanted to let you know that tomorrow we're going cross country skiing in the morning," Norah said. "We have skills in the afternoon, and we'll come down for game night after dinner, but I'll try to keep them as quiet as I can."

"Don't worry about it," Sterling said, ducking his head so he wouldn't have to look at her. "I kinda like having you here. The cabin doesn't feel so…big."

Norah patted his forearm like he was an obedient dog and headed for the stairs. "See you later."

Sterling's skin tingled where she'd touched it, and he trailed his fingers where hers had just been. "Hey, thanks for the food." He watched her wave over her shoulder as she disappeared up the stairs, not quite sure why his stomach squeezed or why he wanted her to stay for a few more minutes. Maybe with his phone so silent, it simply felt good to talk to someone again.

———

By the next evening, Sterling wanted to order pizza again. Norah was not the best of cooks, though she obviously tried hard. But the waffles she served him at breakfast tasted more like salt than anything else, and the soup she'd brought him for lunch was nothing more than water with noodles and overcooked carrots. And the bread? Well, Sterling didn't think *that* was bread.

Sterling took a bite or two before engaging her in whatever conversation he could. She only stayed for a few minutes anyway, as she couldn't leave the girls for long. He'd raided the pantry, eaten all the stale peanut butter crackers his mom kept there, even went so far as to consider making a boxed dinner. He didn't want to hurt Norah's feelings, so he thumbed off his phone and laid it next to him on the couch.

She brought down a pizza box with the girls, ushering them all into the game room while she approached with a literal slice of heaven. "Pizza tonight."

Sterling practically leapt off the couch to get to it.

"Thanks, Norah." He beamed at her, his mouth watering for cheese and pepperoni. "You guys have already eaten?" The box held half a pie.

She giggled, the sound worming past his eardrums and accelerating his heartbeat. "Yeah. That's all yours."

He put his hand on her shoulder, realizing too late the effect that would have on his already fragile emotions. She startled under the weight of his touch, and when their eyes met, something passed between them.

Sterling almost sensed that Norah was as lonely as he was. *Impossible,* he told himself. She had a job surrounded by people. A family who she spent every evening with. Still, with the moments stretching between them, and his stupid hand still on her shoulder, Sterling felt something stir within him.

He cleared his throat and settled his weight away from her. She fell back two steps, her hands sliding up her arms from elbow to shoulder, as if cold. "Okay, well, we'll be down here for a few hours. Hope we don't bother you."

Sterling couldn't quite get his voice to tell her that she certainly didn't bother him. Instead, he lifted a piece of pizza from the box and waved at her. With food in his stomach, he didn't feel so jumpy, but he still wanted to join Norah in the game room and find out everything about her.

Sunday morning, she skipped downstairs to ask him if he wanted to go to church with her and the girls. Sterling hadn't quite known how to answer. His family was religious—the many and varied decorations around the house testified of that. He walked past a picture of Jesus every morning on the way to the bathroom, and a huge glass vase next to the hearth boasted the word "Faith" down the front.

In the end, he'd said no and retreated to his bedroom, where another television and another cooking show held his attention until he heard the girls leave.

Religion was just another way Sterling had rebelled from the perfect, educated, spiritually powerful Maughan family. As he waited for Norah to return, he couldn't help wondering if he would've been spared from the accident had he been more concerned with what God thought about him than what the country thought.

He banished the reminders of Amber, determined not to relive the things she'd said, the way her infidelity had been discovered on live TV because she forgot to remove her mic before meeting up with her secret boyfriend.

Monday, Norah brought down a steaming bowl of spaghetti and a slice of homemade bread for lunch. "Not sure on the bread," she said. "The girls made it—it's part of their treatment. They have to learn new skills to replace their bad habits. Genn made this, and well, she thinks she may have forgotten something."

Sterling eyed the bread, remembering the earlier disaster he'd tasted. Maybe he'd judged Norah prematurely. "Did one of the girls make that bread on Saturday?"

"No, that was my demo loaf. They made theirs today."

Sterling's appetite vanished. If these girls had Norah for a culinary instructor, he didn't hold much hope for this round of bread. "Well, it looks right."

"Well, salt looks like sugar, too." Norah giggled, and Sterling jerked his hand away from the bread.

"You're kidding, right?"

"I honestly don't know." Norah smiled, a warm, happy grin that made Sterling want to figure out if she always felt as joyful as she looked.

"You leaving today?"

"I'm taking the girls back in a few minutes," Norah said. "They have a group therapy session this afternoon. While they're doing that, I'll come back here to clean up."

Sterling's heart pounced against his ribs, for no reason he could name. "I'm probably going to take another nap." He gave her a half-smile, pleased when she rolled her eyes.

"Don't you have physical therapy or something?"

"Yeah," Sterling said. "I do the exercises the doctor told me to." Only for the past three days, but Norah didn't need to know that. "I have to go to Missoula next week for a check-up. Make sure everything's healing right. Whatever." He waved his fork in the air like a magic wand and twirled it in the spaghetti.

Norah put her hand on his shoulder as she stood. He froze, every nerve ending suddenly firing on all cylinders.

She yanked her hand back as if she could feel the increased energy coursing through him. "I hope your recovery continues to go well." She glanced around, her eyes sweeping over surfaces, decorations, and his open bedroom door. "Seems like things have gotten better around here." She spoke like she knew that until she showed up, he hadn't showered in days, hadn't gotten off the couch, hadn't been doing his physical therapy.

"Norah," he said, his voice a tick too thick. "Thank you for this weekend." His stomach might not be so grateful, but his psyche certainly was.

She stared at him, mouth slightly open, those beautiful brown eyes blinking and blinking and blinking. "You're welcome?"

He chuckled, though he wondered why her statement sounded like a question. "I mean it. It's been...nice having you here. So, you know, thanks."

"No problem." She stepped away, and Sterling racked his brain for another topic of conversation. With his mind blank, he flashed her a tight smile and took a bite of the bread—Norah could take lessons from Genn on how to get dough to rise properly.

An hour later, he completed part of his physical therapy as he paced from the huge wall of windows in the living room, through the kitchen, down a hall, and to the game room door and back. He heard the distinct rhythm of wheeled suitcases rolling across the tile upstairs. Out into the garage. The slam of a door, and then silence.

He was alone in the house. Again.

A heaviness descended upon him, one he'd only hinted at before. He hadn't truly understood why talking to Norah meant so much to him, why having her there hadn't been as hard as he'd originally thought.

With everyone gone again, he realized he hated being

alone, more than he hated Amber for cheating on him, more than he hated wearing his leg brace.

———

"Sterling."

He woke to the sound of an angel's voice. An angel with dark, curly hair. Full lips. Worried eyes.

"Norah." He sat up, glad he'd left on the light in the kitchen but noting the pain in his leg and the darkness beyond the blinds he'd opened. "What time is it?"

"About six." She wrung her hands together as Sterling ran his through his hair. "I came back up to clean, and it started snowing. I don't think I can get back down the mountain tonight."

A chill radiated through the room, causing Sterling to rub his hands along his arms. "Why is it so cold?"

"That's why I woke you up," she said. "I think the furnace went out."

He noticed Norah wore her winter coat, her gloves, and a scarf. He stood, testing his weight on his injured leg though he wore his brace. He'd finally started doing the exercises his doctor wanted, but it only seemed to enflame the pain.

"I tried to relight the pilot on the furnace, but couldn't." Norah looked at him, her eyes asking him for another idea.

"Let's build a fire then." He honestly had no idea where the furnace was located in the cabin and was impressed she did. There were probably two, and he'd have to text his dad to find out where they were.

Satisfied he wouldn't fall, he hobbled over to the wood closet behind the fireplace. "There's matches in the kitchen," he said. "They're in the cupboard above the microwave. Grab 'em, will you?"

Her footsteps scuffled away while he heaved a couple pieces of wood into his arms. "Oh, and there's some lunch bags in the pantry. Grab those too." Thankfully, his mother kept everything stocked even when the house wasn't being used. He'd made enough peanut butter sandwiches for his nieces and nephews to know about the brown bags.

She collected the matches and the paper sacks while he bit back a groan of pain as he knelt to construct a lean-to in the fireplace. He needed a painkiller, fast, but pushed past the stiffness and pain, hoping Norah hadn't noticed.

He crumpled a few bags, stuffing them into the spaces beneath the wood. A few match strikes later, and smoke began to rise from the wood. But it didn't go up the chimney; it started to fill the room.

He mumbled under his breath as Norah coughed and he fumbled to locate the flue. He pulled the lever, and a few minutes later, the smoke had dispersed as the flames built and roared and crackled with heavy amounts of heat.

"There," he said, satisfied that he'd *done something.* "We can stay warm right here."

Norah's panicked gaze flew to his. "We?"

He took a few steps to the windows and looked out at the thick blanket of white obscuring the sky. "It's coming down hard. No way you can drive in that. Unless you have a truck?"

One glance in her direction, and he knew she didn't. Probably a little four-door sedan that weighed less than he did.

"I have some leftover soup upstairs," Norah said, practically running for the stairs.

"Okay." Sterling watched her go, wondering why she was so nervous. A tremor of excitement stirred inside him—maybe a bit of dread at having to choke down that bland soup.

But now that Norah couldn't leave—now that she couldn't retreat to the unheated upper floors—he could learn more about her.

CHAPTER 3

*N*orah fisted her hands and stuck them in her pockets while she stood in front of the fridge in the upstairs kitchen. The cold descending on the house made her teeth chatter, but the handsome man downstairs was really the reason her insides quaked.

The man who'd just built a fire and invited her to stay in the basement with him.

Pipes, ran through her mind. Didn't he need to fix the furnace so the pipes didn't freeze? Maybe people like the Maughans didn't care about that. Maybe they just forked over thousands of dollars to fix broken pipes and iced furnaces.

Norah finally reached for the bowl of leftover soup and pulled out the half-loaf of bread the girls hadn't eaten. When she'd realized how cold the house was, she'd left her bags by the garage door and stopped packing the food and supplies.

The snow falling outside the windows made for zero visibility. She'd driven in dozens of storms, but nothing this dense. Snow like this kept everyone off the roads, indoors with generators at the ready, and Norah had never felt so trapped before.

As she thought about spending this storm with Sterling, the two feet of snow suddenly seemed magical, looked soft as it swirled to the ground like fairy wings. Norah took a deep breath and activated her phone so she could call home.

After explaining about the weather to Javier, she put in a call to Silver Creek, where the night manager told her to stay safe and get down the mountain when she could.

With nothing keeping her upstairs, Norah had no choice but to go down. The heat licking up the stairs bathed her face in warmth, and she sighed despite the tight knot her stomach had become.

"Soup," she announced as she stepped into the room. Sterling had closed all the blinds, but she didn't see him in the living room or kitchen. His scuffled steps came from the other side of the house, near the game room. A door closed. Scuffle-step. Scuffle-step. Another door closed.

Norah put the soup in the microwave and pressed a button. She turned and saw the small army of pill bottles. She recognized some of the names, but one in particular caught her eye. Just one of those pills would give her so much relief—an hour of bliss, free from worry, from her constant struggles. Sterling would never miss just one.

"I closed all the doors down here to keep the heat contained." Sterling came around the corner, his square jaw and strong shoulders reminding Norah why she'd enjoyed seeing him snowboard during the Olympics, why she'd unconsciously smile at his picture when she dusted, why she'd patiently endured sitting with Javier as he watched Sterling's recorded interviews late at night after Mama had gone to bed.

Her fingers twitched toward the bottle, and she consciously fisted them to keep them away from the painkillers.

"I left the bathroom door open so we won't freeze in there, and checked the furnace in the game room. You're right. Pilot light won't light." Sterling glanced over his shoulder toward the bathroom closest to the living room. "My dad said to call someone in the morning." A flash of pain stole across his face, but he wiped it away quickly.

"Great." Norah sliced the bread so she wouldn't have to look at Sterling—or the pill bottle. But that only took five seconds, and she found her gaze wandering back to his. He couldn't seem to look away from her either, and something charged passed between them. That same something that leapt from his body to hers earlier when she'd touched his shoulder.

Something Norah couldn't have identified even if she tried. She hadn't dated in years—since Mama's diagnosis. She simply didn't have time, didn't want to talk about herself or her family or her past. She didn't want the bother.

But for Sterling Maughan, Norah wondered if the trouble might be worth the prize.

He cleared his throat, and she dropped her eyes to the knife she still held.

"I got out a bunch of blankets." He gestured toward the large, sectional couch, giving her somewhere safe to look. "My mom keeps quite the movie collection here at the cabin. And we have more than enough wood to get through the night." He indicated the closet around the corner, behind the fireplace, which had overflowed with timber when he'd opened it earlier. "We'll survive. We might just have to…conserve body heat."

A blush flamed in Norah's face, and she spun back to the microwave. "And I have soup and bread." She pasted on a smile before she twisted to face him. She could play the non-awkward part to near perfection. Over the years, she'd had a lot of practice with Mama's boyfriends.

He moved to the couch and sat way down on one end. She handed him a bowl of soup and turned to the TV. "What should we watch?"

"Whatever you want."

She looked through the titles in the built-in drawer, seeing her usual favorites—romantic comedies. No way was she watching one of those with such athletic male perfection perched nearby. She chose an action superhero flick and slid the disc into the player.

Sterling manned the remotes while Norah sat on the opposite end of the L-shaped couch. Her back faced the windows, and a chill swept across her neck though she was positioned closest to the fire, which put out plenty of heat.

She kept the chill at bay while she sipped the soup, but

once she finished, the cold penetrated her defenses. She rose and moved to the middle of the couch, directly in front of the fire and just one place away from Sterling.

"It's cold over there," she murmured by way of explanation, feeling the weight of Sterling's gaze on her face. She turned and met his eyes, so full of questions and something else…something that looked like emotion. What kind of emotion, Norah couldn't name.

"Can you hand me one of those blankets?" he asked, his arms crossed stiffly across his chest and light from the movie flickering on his face.

"Sure." She reached for one of the quilts he'd stacked in the corner of the couch. She spread the blanket over him, their hands brushing as she did. She felt the solidness of his shoulder, his arm, and his leg as she carefully tucked the blanket around his brace.

"There."

"Thank you," he said, those two words painting glorious pictures in her mind. Very few people expressed thanks to her—especially not someone like Sterling. She eyed him, wondering what other surprises he had to give, wondering what kind of man he really was.

He watched the movie for a couple of minutes before he said, "There's hot chocolate in the pantry."

"Are you saying you want hot chocolate?" Norah smiled and a rush of warmth filled her face when he grinned back.

"Definitely."

She busied herself in the kitchen, wishing she could sort through her scrambled emotions, wishing that small, orange bottle didn't sing so strongly to her. She cleared her throat, wishing her mind could be as easily purged.

"Hey, there's a counselor job opening at the center." She slid two mugs of milk into the microwave. "Do you think you might be interested?"

He turned down the volume on the movie. "Counseling addicted teens?" His voice held more disbelief than interest.

"I told my boss you were a cop too. He thinks you might be a good fit for our at-risk boys."

Sterling harrumphed, a sound that set Norah's nerves on edge. She hadn't expected him to dismiss the idea so quickly. Maybe not apply instantly, but at least entertain the notion.

"I'm not really into addicts."

Norah's heart seized. Of course he wasn't. No respectable man would want a woman with a drug history, least of all Sterling Maughan. Norah couldn't clear the raging waves of hurt from her throat, which was just plain stupid. It wasn't like she and Sterling were even together.

"It's more than just addicts." Her voice came out like the Gold Valley wind, sharp and biting. She swallowed to tame it back into niceness. "Our at-risk boys usually come from gangs, and Doctor Richards likes their counselors to have experience in law enforcement or the military." Norah shrugged, as if Sterling could see her with his back turned. "It's okay if you're not interested."

"Do I have to ride a horse?"

"No," Norah said as she pulled out the mugs. "But it's

always helpful if the counselors have some experience with animals."

"Do you?"

She mixed the chocolate powder with the milk. "Yes, I took the center's basic riding classes when I started there a couple of years ago. I don't do much riding, though. The girls like the time away from me, I think." She gave a light laugh, thinking of the girls in her group right now. All good girls who'd just gotten caught up in bad things.

Norah tested the taste and temperature of one mug of hot chocolate, thinking of her own run-in with a dangerous substance. She was still a good person. A good person who'd gotten caught up in something bad.

"Mm." She gave the other mug a final stir and took them both to the couch. She handed one to Sterling, who wrapped his fingers around the warm ceramic, his eyes never leaving hers.

"You really think I could be a counselor?"

Norah smiled at the uncertainty in his voice. "Sure, why not?"

A dark look crossed his face. "A lot of reasons." He took a sip of his hot chocolate, startling away from the mug and making a face. When he caught her watching, he pinned a grin in place. "Hot." He chuckled. "So tell me more about the at-risk boys."

Norah grinned, tucked her feet under her, covered herself with a blanket, and took a sip of her hot chocolate—not too hot and not too cold. "They're probably a lot like you…."

———

Sterling could listen to Norah talk all day and all night. Her voice had a soothing quality he liked, that her girls probably appreciated. He found himself sinking into the warmth of it, but that could've been the hot chocolate, though that was neither hot nor chocolaty.

Probably the painkiller, he thought. He'd downed one while Norah was upstairs getting the soup. The screaming pain in his leg had urged him to throw back the whole bottle, but the white-hot agony had now settled into a dull ache.

After she finished telling him about the at-risk boys—who didn't sound like more than Officer Maughan could handle—he sighed. "I haven't been a cop for a while, Norah." Sterling cursed the soft way he spoke her name, sure it had given away too much.

"That's okay," she said, her voice a bit too masked. "You have the training, and some experience, and it's like riding a bike, right?"

Sterling hadn't ridden a bike for a while either, but agreed with Norah. The idea of working with at-risk boys actually appealed to him. He could be a positive role model, the way he had been as a cop, the way he had as a professional snowboarder who didn't party and drink and go home with groupies.

"I'm sure you can talk someone down, or keep calm in a stressful situation." She took his nearly full mug and set it next to hers on the coffee table. "There's a meeting next weekend at the center. You could meet Doctor Richards and ask any other questions you have. Find out more, no strings attached."

Sterling focused on the movie, though he hadn't watched a single minute of it. He'd been consumed by watching Norah lift her soup spoon to her lips, then enthralled when she moved closer to him. The tenderness and compassion with which she helped him suggested her experience as a caretaker.

He needed something to do all day, and maybe learning to ride a horse could be it. Maybe he should learn more about working at Silver Creek.

"I don't have a car to get to the meeting," he said. "And I'm not supposed to drive."

"I could come get you." She waved her hand like that problem had been solved. "I brought an application for you, just in case you were interested."

He swung his gaze toward her. "What made you think I'd be interested?"

She picked at something invisible on her quilt, then adjusted it higher to cover her shoulders. "I don't know. You seemed…. I don't know."

"No, go on," he said. "I seemed what?"

She focused on something in the kitchen. "You seemed lost when I met you on Friday. I know about your snowboarding—everyone watched you win the gold medal last year—and to see you in that nest of blankets…."

Sterling cringed. So she'd noticed. Noticed everything

he'd hoped she hadn't. "I washed those blankets, just so you know. Sprayed air freshener too."

Norah blinked, then burst into laughter. She stood and took their mugs and soup bowls into the kitchen. "Trust me, I get it."

"You do?"

"Sure." She returned to the couch, flopping into her spot, which lingered just out of Sterling's reach. "You've been injured, and your life has changed. It's okay, you know, to feel angry, or hurt, or depressed right now. No one's expecting you to be happy about what's happened."

Sterling stared at his hands on top of the blanket. His parents expected him to *get happy* about what had happened. His mother said God had a plan for him, and it simply wasn't snowboarding. That he needed to get as healthy as possible, and then figure out what God wanted him to do.

Her lecture had only fanned the flames of anger in Sterling's chest. *He* wanted to snowboard. Why did God get to decide what Sterling did with his life?

"Would you be angry, or hurt, or depressed if something like this happened to you?" he whispered, sure Norah wouldn't answer.

"Of course." She didn't sound ashamed or worried about what he'd think. Sterling wondered if he would ever be able to talk about snowboarding and his accident in such an even tone.

"You'll get better. This isn't forever." She scooted closer and put her hand on his, her slender fingers slipping between his, creating a piano-like array of black and white. "It might take a while. But you'll have help from your family and friends."

He looked at her, fell right into the depths of her eyes, got lost in the sincerity of her tone, enjoyed the warmth of her hand in his. "Tell me about your family."

Her fingers tightened and then released. She straightened, putting more inches between them. "My family is… well, they're doing the best they can."

Sterling sensed a note of finality in her words, so he didn't push her any further. His family was probably doing the best they could too. His brothers had called and sent cards, flowers, and gifts. Rex had helped Sterling when he got discharged from the hospital. He'd driven him up to the cabin, stocked the house with frozen burritos and boxes of cereal, and checked in from time to time.

Still, Sterling didn't see any of them here with him, talking to him like his negative and bitter feelings were normal, his struggles real, his injuries a terrible injustice. His mother would never even suggest such things. It wasn't okay to be angry. He never could tell her about ideas or problems he wrestled with. In the Maughan household, tears weren't tolerated, questions discouraged. And she'd already said his injuries were meant to put him on the right path in life.

If only he knew what path that was, and why God cared so little about him that He had to shatter Sterling's left leg and steal his future to get him there.

CHAPTER 4

$\mathcal{N}$orah shivered, the uncomfortable sensation tearing her away from unconsciousness. Absolute darkness prevailed, and she couldn't tell if her eyes were open or not.

She blinked, trying to figure out what had gone wrong. "The fire."

Sterling's steady breathing sounded to her right, and Norah fumbled for her cell phone, which she'd left on the coffee table. Her fingers touched it, but she could barely curl them around the phone, cold as they were.

Her teeth shook and a violent shiver wracked her shoulders. She thumbed on the phone, squinting against the sudden bright light. She turned on the flashlight and aimed it at the fireplace.

Out.

Norah moved to kneel in front of the hearth, taking several pieces of wood from the pile Sterling had stacked the night before. He'd left the paper bags and matches nearby, and she worked as quickly as she could with trembling hands.

A few minutes later, a friendly flame flickered in the firebox. Norah grabbed her quilt from the couch and wrapped it around her shoulders as she repositioned herself in front of the flames. A moment later, she realized she was hogging all the heat.

She returned to the couch, where she slipped the blanket around to cover her as she snuggled into Sterling's left side, careful not to jostle his injured leg. His body emanated warmth, and a final shiver shook Norah's body as a quick fantasy of him cradling her against his chest flashed through her mind.

She shook away the ridiculous images, erased the slight smile that had upturned her lips, and closed her eyes. The next time she woke, pale orange light colored the room. She got up and added another log to the fire. Once it became friends with the other flames, she stood and listened to the wind howling outside. Doubts crept into her mind about when she'd be able to get back to the valley.

"Norah?"

She twisted toward the sound of Sterling's voice. The firelight painted his face in handsome lines, and Norah's breath caught. "Yeah?"

"You okay?"

"Just adding wood to the fire. And listening to the wind."

Sterling cocked his head to the side, obviously listening. "Sounds like the storm's still going strong."

Norah returned to her spot on the couch, wishing she could cuddle up with Sterling again, and brought her knees to her chest. A thread of horror stole through her when she thought of him knowing she'd snuggled into him for warmth.

She cast him a sneak peek out of the corner of her eye. Did he know she'd used him for warmth in the middle of the night?

He didn't seem to know.

"How long can we survive up here?" she asked to calm her rampant thoughts.

Sterling reached for his phone and grunted as he moved his leg. A groan followed, a low, deep sound that spoke only of pain.

"Let me get your pills." She stepped into the kitchen, using her phone's flashlight to get his medicine and fill a glass with water. She stalled with the bottle of hydrocodone in her hand, remembering her own pain, her own path with this drug. Time seemed to stretch just as it had when she'd been under the influence of this drug.

She shook herself and centered her thoughts. She tapped one pill into her palm and returned to Sterling.

He took the medicine with agony reflecting in his eyes. "Thank you." He laid his head back and sighed. "It's not even five," he said. "Too early to be awake."

"Whatever, Sleeping Beauty," Norah said. "You fell asleep by nine."

"I'm *recovering*." A curve tugged against his lips, his eyes still shut. Norah stared at him unabashedly. She'd expected his rugged good looks to unseat her—they had through a television screen.

She hadn't expected him to be soft-spoken, grateful, or interested in anything but himself. But last night, he'd asked question after question about her family, the job at Silver Creek, and her social work classes. When she'd asked about his family, she sensed his sadness. If she understood anything, it was that pictures didn't always tell the whole story. In fact, the numerous family photos around Six Sons Cabin probably masked the truth more than revealed it.

He'd given a little information about his father's class on real estate investing in Madagascar and his brothers who lived around the country. He obviously adored his nieces and nephews. Norah had heard as much in his voice.

"You never said how long we could survive up here," she said, hoping to get outside her tumbling thoughts.

"Forever," he said. "When I got here last week, my brother hauled in a ton of groceries. And my mom always keeps the cabin well-stocked." He yawned. "We'll be fine for at least a couple weeks."

A couple weeks. In a snowbound luxury cabin. A couple weeks in a snowbound luxury cabin with a dreamy sports star. Norah shouldn't feel so freaked out by such a prospect. Any single woman with a pair of operational eyes would be delighted.

She snuck another glance at Sterling, but he hadn't moved. His chest rose and fell in even breaths, her signal that he'd drifted back to sleep. The silence unnerved her further, if that were even possible. She got up and went in the bathroom, just to find a space to think that didn't scream *Sterling!*

If she wanted such a place, the bathroom Sterling had been using wasn't it. His razor, shaving cream, and after-shave sat on the counter. His clothes were stacked in the linen cupboard.

With the budding light from the window, she saw herself in the mirror, the disheveled appearance of her hair sending a shock through her. She combed her fingers through the curls and yearned for her toiletries and a fresh set of clothes. Moving as quietly as possible, she snuck upstairs to where she'd left her suitcase and brought it downstairs.

Sterling didn't move, not even a twitch, and Norah envied the drug-induced sleep he'd fallen into as she brushed her teeth and tamed her curls.

———

By mid-morning, the snow ceased. Only an hour later, the rumbling sound of snowplows reached Norah's ears. Sterling had banked the fire and called the furnace repairman by the time Norah loaded her car with her belongings.

She sighed in relief and frustration as she started the trip down the mountain. The time with Sterling should've been pleasant—they spoke of her classes, his future in snow-boarding, and managed to make lunch in the same kitchen with nothing but smiles and easy conversation.

She hated that she felt so tight during that time, that she hadn't let herself enjoy being with him.

"You've got to relax," she chastised herself as she eased the sedan around a corner. Countless women would've liked to have been in her place.

It took her twenty minutes to reach the valley. She continued past Silver Creek and into town, where the snowplows had also been hard at work.

She crossed into the older part of town, where her childhood home waited with three feet of new snow in the driveway. She didn't see footprints, which meant her brothers had been cooped up in the house with Mama—and each other—all day.

Exhaustion weighed on her as she stopped on the street and climbed out of the car. Would it have killed her almost eighteen-year-old brother to get out the shovel and clear the driveway? If shoveling snow wouldn't kill him, Javier should've known Norah would when she got home.

Norah tromped to the garage and kicked the snow away so she could lift the door. She slammed it up, making more noise than necessary. Her passive-aggressive fit worked; Javier poked his head out the door that led to the kitchen.

"Hey, Norah."

She glared in his direction as she grabbed the snow shovel with exaggerated force.

"I was gonna get to it," he said.

"Right," she muttered as she dug the shovel into the snow. A few minutes later, all three of her brothers joined her, Javier wielding a second shovel while Alex used a broom to push the snow out of the way and Erik followed them all with a bag of salt.

"You know, you're not going to live here forever," Norah said to Javier as Alex and Erik moved down the sidewalk toward the front door.

"I know."

"Who do you think is going to take care of your apartment? Your driveway?" Norah straightened to relieve the pain in her lower back. Sleeping on a couch hadn't helped, even if it was the most expensive couch on the planet.

"I don't know," Javier mumbled, lifting another shovelful of snow and tossing it onto the pile.

"Javier." Her serious tone did the trick. He stopped working and looked at her. "I want more for you," she said. "You have to do more than Mama. More than me." She gestured to the house. "You have to get out of here." Tears pricked her eyes, bringing some welcome heat to her face. "Stay clean. Stay away from girls. And get out of here."

Javier nodded and dug the shovel into the snow again. "Okay, Norah."

"Promise me, Javier." She put her gloved hand on his arm and met his eye again.

"Norah, I've promised you this a million times."

"Then one more time won't hurt."

Javier rolled his eyes. "I promise. No girls. No drugs. Get good grades. Get out of Gold Valley."

Norah nodded, even though his promise was delivered in a monotone, and continued working. With the driveway and front sidewalk cleared and salted, Norah pulled her car into the garage.

"Thanks, guys," she said. Her three half-brothers gave her guilty smiles as they entered the house. "How's Mama?"

"She's havin' a bad day," Erik, the youngest at only ten, said. "Something broke in her room, but she won't let nobody in there."

Norah didn't have to look very hard to see what her brothers had been doing all day: video games. The pot that held the remains of their lunch—macaroni and cheese— waited for her on the stove.

"Homework?"

"Already done," Javier said. "No school today either, so we're all caught up."

Norah nodded and cast her eyes down the hall that led to their mama's room. The door sat shut. She didn't want to break the seal protecting her from her mother right now. Just being in the run-down house with walls that needed fresh paint, carpet that had long lost its ability to come clean, a tiny kitchen in need of new countertops and cupboards, reminded her of what different worlds she and Sterling came from.

Not to mention his comment about not being into addicts.

You're not an addict, a voice whispered in her head. She'd been clean for eleven years, even if the painkillers called to her from time to time. Still, she didn't want Sterling to know her first experience with Silver Creek had been as one of its patients.

He'd stood and thanked her when she'd prepared to leave. His awkward hug still lingered on her shoulders, the masculine scent of him still stuck to her skin. That magnetic force had sparked between them again, but it was easy to dismiss when confronted with her real life.

And she would never show Sterling her real life.

Taking a deep breath, which she immediately regretted due to the musty smell that came with the air, she stepped down the hall. She knocked on Mama's bedroom door as she opened it, and found a broken picture frame on the floor two steps inside the room.

Norah bent to pick it up, sliding the picture out from under the broken glass. It was her father, the only man Mama had actually married. He'd died when Norah was a toddler, and that had started her mother down a path of endless boyfriends. Norah had determined by age ten—when Javier came along—that she wouldn't fall victim to a man's charms, ever. And marriage? Wasn't in the cards for Norah.

"Mama?" Norah collected the bigger pieces of glass and balanced them on the photograph.

Mama slept slightly reclined against the headboard, her tiny TV flickering in the darkness. She didn't answer, so Norah quietly cleaned up the broken picture frame and took the glass out to the garage trashcan.

When she returned to Mama's room, she checked the pill bottle on the nightstand. The appropriate number of anti-depressants had been taken. No more, no less. A breath of relief released from her lungs, and she smoothed Mama's dark, silky hair off her forehead.

She stepped out of the room, wondering what had

prompted Mama to get out her only husband's picture and shatter it against the door.

She'd stopped trying to figure out her mother by age fifteen—about the same time Erik's dad introduced her to hydrocodone for her frequent migraines. She liked the way the pills made it so she didn't worry about Mama, didn't think about what Mama would say or do, didn't make her wonder if she'd ever be free. She started taking them when she didn't have a headache, simply to escape her own mind.

The pull to find a bottle of painkillers and swallow a handful yanked at her resolve, and Norah joined her brothers in the living room to remind herself of what she'd worked so hard to overcome. Besides the twelve weeks at Silver Creek, she'd spent months trying to figure out how to deal with her life in appropriate ways.

Ways that included school, and work, and raising Javier, Alex, and Erik. She couldn't let them down. She wouldn't.

Her eleven-year-long clean streak still intact, Norah sat next to Javier and watched her brothers play video games. Her mind wandered to Sterling, and what he was doing tonight, if he might be sitting on his couch, thinking about her.

———

Sterling hadn't gotten Norah's phone number before she left on Monday afternoon, a fact he cursed himself for until Thursday morning. Then he stopped brooding and looked up the number for the Silver Creek Rehabilitation Center.

He dialed, his heart ba-booming in his chest. He wasn't used to asking for help, and certainly not from a pretty woman who'd curled into his side to keep warm during a snowstorm. He'd been thinking for three straight days about the scent of her skin, the softness of her breath against his arm, the way her body tremored next to his until she warmed up.

"Silver Creek."

"Hey, is Norah Watson there?" Sterling's throat stuck on her name, and he swallowed.

"She's in crafts with the girls. Can I take a message?"

Sterling pressed his eyes closed. "Yeah, this is Sterling Maughan. She gave me an application for a job there, and I need to get in touch with her. Can you have her call me?" He gave the receptionist his cell number, and hung up with the assurance that Norah would call when she got a chance.

He'd barely touched the door to the game room when his phone chimed, and he spun, dozens of feet between him and Norah's call. At least he hoped it was her. No one besides Rex had called, and he usually didn't phone until evening.

He'd kept up with his physical therapy, and he'd noticed a vast improvement in his leg, but it didn't make the distance seem any less intimidating. Sterling half hopped, half jogged into the living room, swiping open the call a heartbeat before it went to voicemail. "Hello?"

"Sterling, it's Norah."

He tried to catch his breath, but his heart pumped out an

extra beat at the sound of her voice. "Hey." A smile crossed his face, leaked into his voice.

"You called about the application?"

"Oh, yeah, I wondered what time that meeting was on Saturday? You said you could come get me…. I checked the weather and it's supposed to be clear skies." He pinched his eyes closed for a moment before opening them again. He moved to the windows, where he'd opened all the blinds to let in the sunlight.

"Sure, I can come." The shuffling of papers came through the line. "The meeting is on Saturday at three." Norah's exhale came through the line, a sound like a closing door, and then a sigh. "It should last about an hour. Sometimes longer."

"Do you work on Saturday?"

"Not at Silver Creek."

Curiosity gnawed at Sterling. "How many jobs do you have?"

"Two." Her clipped tone suggested he stop asking questions. Now. He didn't want to stop; he wanted to know everything about her.

"Cleaning houses?" he asked.

"Yes," she said. "I have a dozen clients up in the cabins."

He wondered why she needed to work two jobs, but he managed to keep the inquiry to himself. "Will it be too hard to take me to the meeting?"

"No," she said. "I'll be up there anyway."

"We can go to dinner after the meeting." The words flew from Sterling's mouth before he'd even thought them.

The silence coming through the line reeked of surprise. The same emotion coursed through Sterling's body.

"I mean, if you want." Sterling coughed and stepped onto the deck so the cold air could clear his mind. "Do you want to go to dinner with me, Norah?"

Sterling hoped with every bone in his body that she'd say yes. He'd missed her these past three days; his loneliness felt like a tangible presence in the cabin. The nurse only stayed for a few minutes, only asked questions about his leg, his medicine. And she'd said that morning that she didn't need to come every day anymore.

"I, well—" Norah started and then stopped.

Sterling waited, the pause growing uncomfortable after only two breaths. "It's okay," he said at the same time she said, "Sure, let's go to dinner."

Relief rammed into Sterling at the brightness of her words, making his feet unsteady. He reached for the sliding glass door to balance himself. "Great," he said, another smile infusing his voice. "Have you been to Migliano's? They have the best crab cakes in town."

"I've never been." Norah sounded withdrawn now, her words barely registering in his ears.

"Do you like Italian? They have pizza and pasta and all that normal stuff too."

"I'm sure it's great," she said. "And yes, I like Italian."

"Great." Sterling wanted to add, *Because I like you,* but he bit back the flirty remark. He had a feeling Norah wouldn't respond well to it, and he didn't want to be the same man he'd been on the snowboarding circuit.

That man had died when he'd fallen off a mountain, and Sterling had mourned him for a while. But now…. Now he was ready to be someone else. Who, he wasn't quite sure, but when he imagined himself with Norah at his side, he wasn't holding a snowboard.

"See you Saturday," he said, glad when she confirmed in her normal joyful tone, and hung up. Now if only he didn't have to suffer through fifty hours until he saw another human being again.

No, not just another human being.

Sterling didn't want to wait another minute to see *Norah*.

CHAPTER 5

"Come in!" Sterling had already made the climb up the stairs. It hadn't taken him as long as it had that first time. He'd thought about going to the meeting without his leg brace, but he'd tried doing his walking exercises that morning without it, and he'd paid a hefty price by needing two painkillers and a long nap before his hip stopped throbbing.

Norah cracked the door leading into the house from the garage, the entrance he'd told her to use. "Hey, you're looking good." She grinned at him, scanning him from head to toe and back.

"You think I'm good-looking?" He kicked a smile in her direction.

"Me and all of America." She laughed, unaware of the rush of happiness soaring through Sterling, not only from her infectious laugh, but because he felt anything but good-looking with the bulky leg brace and pronounced limp.

"You're getting around better," she commented as he took the three steps up to the door.

"I guess my doctor knows what he's talking about." He opened the door. "Shall we?"

She took a deep breath and nodded. "I brought something to change into for dinner." She indicated her red sweater and skinny jeans. "Something nicer than this."

"That would be fine," he said, his voice rough and thick as he tried not to soak in the curves of her body. "You look great." He ducked his head as he entered the garage. He stopped at the top of the stairs. "Hey, can you go in front of me?"

She squeezed past him, infusing his air with the sweet scent of her perfume. Something with fruit or flowers. Maybe both.

He used the rail for balance, but with Norah in front of him, he didn't feel like he could spill forward at any moment.

"Thank you," he said when he reached the bottom. He slid his hand down her forearm to her fingers and squeezed once before letting go. He wondered if she'd let him hold her hand for longer than a heartbeat during dinner. He swallowed just thinking about it. She stared after him as he moved the passenger seat all the way back and folded himself into the car. By the time he'd buckled, a fine bead of sweat had broken out on his hairline.

"This is harder than I thought," he admitted as she turned out of the driveway onto the road. He gave a nervous chuckle. "Sitting on the couch is much easier."

Every bump and turn sent a shock of discomfort through his knee. He gritted his teeth and gripped the armrest. By the time they arrived at Silver Creek, Sterling felt like riding in a car was a new torture device.

Norah helped him stand, and he kept his hold on her hand when she started to move away. "Can you take on a third job?"

Her eyebrows drew down. "What do you mean?"

"I have to get out of that house," he said. "I'm going insane up there alone. I need a babysitter, someone to take me to the park, or the movies, or anything outside of those walls." He slid a sly smile in her direction. "You up for the job?"

"I don't know, Sterling...." She trailed off, looked away, and hugged her arms around herself. "I have class two nights a week, and I, well." She brought her gaze back to his. "I take care of my three half-brothers and my mom all by myself."

His eyebrows shot up. "You do?" New respect for her bloomed in his chest. "I didn't know that. I'm sorry. Is your mom sick?"

Norah moved away from the car, leaving Sterling to follow. She matched her pace to his, never making him feel like his stunted gait was a problem.

"Yes, she has a debilitating lung disease. COPD?" Norah glanced at him, but Sterling didn't know what COPD was. "She doesn't leave the house."

"Oh, well, I could come to your house."

She burst into laughter, but not the same happy sound

he'd heard before. More like doubtful and scared. "You are *not* coming to my house."

"Why not?"

"The whole thing could fit into your basement."

"I don't care."

"Sure, you don't."

Sterling didn't understand the venom in her voice, and couldn't answer because they'd arrived at the meeting and a brown-haired, eager-eyed man met him at the door. "You must be Officer Maughan." The man pumped Sterling's hand. "I'm so glad our Norah got you here."

He looked at her, but she refused to meet his eye, instead wandering further into the room and choosing a seat. "Me too."

"I'm Doctor Richards. Let me know if you have any questions after the meeting." He bustled away, and Sterling entered the room and sat next to Norah on the last row. The meeting started, leaving the worries about what she meant about him caring what size her house was to fly from one side of his mind to the other.

As he listened to Dr. Richards talk about the in-patient mentor program at Silver Creek, a warm feeling descended on Sterling. He'd felt this sensation before, with his family when he was a child, when the eight of them would gather for dinner. When he'd told the truth about breaking his mother's Thanksgiving china. When he used to go to church.

Emotion gathered in his throat, and Sterling knew he was in the right place, doing the right thing.

When Dr. Richards concluded, the group moved outside to the horse stables. A burly man wearing a cowboy hat greeted them, calling himself Owen.

"We encourage anyone applying at Silver Creek to come take riding lessons," Owen said, and that same comforting feeling dove through Sterling again.

He glanced at Norah. "Forget about babysitting. Maybe you could bring me down for riding lessons?"

"Does this mean you're going to apply?" she whispered, her eyes trained on Owen.

"Yeah," he said, his emotion getting lost in the hushed tone. Thank goodness. "I'm going to apply."

———

Norah watched as Sterling wiped his face, but he didn't seem upset or emotional. Maybe his leg hurt from standing for the past twenty minutes while Owen talked about the equine therapy program at Silver Creek.

Her stomach had been in knots since she woke that morning, and she'd skipped breakfast and lunch. What had she been thinking? Accepting Sterling's dinner invitation? Just the jeans he wore cost more than her car. He outclassed her in every sense of the word, and she suspected anyone with one good eye could see right through her carefully crafted façade to make him think she was his equal.

The very idea was laughable. Just like his suggestion of coming to her house. His apartment in Denver had been twice as big and ten times nicer, with stainless steel appliances and hardwood floors. She knew; Javier had watched the in-home interview Sterling had done for Fox Sports just after he won the gold medal at least a dozen times.

No way she was taking him to her house. No way, no how, not ever.

If only she didn't hear him telling her *thank you* in the soft moments before she fell asleep. If only she didn't want to spend every waking minute with him, tell him all her secrets, including the one about her own past addiction. She swallowed the words as Owen finished his presentation.

"So, will you?" Sterling asked as the other attendees moved to ask questions or leave.

"Will I what?"

"Bring me down to riding lessons." Sterling focused on the beautiful black horse standing behind Owen, and he took a step in that direction. Norah followed him, glad for the distraction so she didn't have to answer his question, introducing him to Owen when they arrived at the horse stall.

"Nice to meet you." Owen shook hands with Sterling, and he nodded to the horse.

"What's his name?"

"Blackjack." Owen patted the horse's cheek. "You gonna come to riding lessons?"

"Yes," Sterling said. "I'm still working on getting a ride." He gestured to his leg. "I can't really drive yet."

"I can—" Owen started.

"I'll take you," Norah practically shouted over the wrangler, causing both Owen and Sterling to turn toward her.

Sterling grinned, something devilish residing in his dark eyes. "Perfect."

Norah felt like throwing up, but having Owen pick up and drop off Sterling was somehow worse. She turned away from him to pat Blackjack. "Yeah, perfect."

Sterling pressed in close to her. "If you can't drive me, it's no problem. Owen seemed like he was going to offer."

"I can do it," Norah said without looking at him.

"I'll pay for your gas."

"That would be great."

"Sterling." Dr. Richards' voice sounded behind them, and Sterling stepped away. She'd need to figure out how to breathe with him around, because she couldn't keep holding her breath. The last thing she needed was to pass out while driving him home because he smelled so good.

"Any questions?"

"No," Sterling said. "I'm ready to apply. Norah's going to bring me down for riding lessons."

Norah turned when he said her name. He'd said it a few times, always soft, like she deserved special treatment. She loved hearing him say her name.

"That's great," Dr. Richards said. "How do you feel about the at-risk program? The boys are tougher, more street-wise." Dr. Richards drew Sterling away as they chattered, and Norah watched them go.

She retrieved her dress from the car and went into the bathroom to change. She texted Sterling that she'd meet him in the car whenever he was ready, and tied her trench coat around her dress.

She'd almost made it out the front door when another counselor came through it. Lori whistled at Norah's red heels. "Where are you off to?"

"Nowhere," Norah lied, clutching the coat tighter.

Lori raised one eyebrow, something Norah usually appreciated—when it was directed at someone else. "Looks like you have a date."

Norah allowed herself to smile. "Maybe I do."

"Norah!" Lori squealed and rushed her, batting away her hands and opening the coat so she could see the little black dress Norah had pulled from the back of her closet.

"Oh, honey, you look fantastic. Who's the lucky guy?"

"Just some guy I met last week." Norah heard the false tone in her voice. Sterling was anything but "some guy."

"You must really like him. I've never known you to go out with anyone."

And Lori would know, because her brother had been interested in Norah the previous summer, and Norah had turned him down over and over. And over. Guilt still needled her about that from time to time.

"He's okay." Norah shrugged. "It's our first date." She pulled her coat closed and buttoned it. "Please don't make a big deal about it."

Lori shook her blonde head. "Oh, it's a big deal! Norah, when did you decide to date again?" Only concern rode in her friend's voice, or Norah would've been annoyed.

"I haven't, not really."

Lori looked down at the three-inch red heels with the bow-embellished strap. "Um, this looks like you've decided to start dating again. I thought you didn't want to get married."

"I don't." And Norah didn't feel bad for speaking that truth.

Lori appraised her, and Norah didn't like the disbelief in her friend's eyes. "I'll call you later, okay?"

Lori brightened. "Promise?"

Norah giggled. "You have a boyfriend. I don't know why you're so interested in this."

"We've been together too long," Lori said. "I'm thinking about breaking up with him."

"You are?" Norah stalled in her escape, one hand on the doorknob.

Tears shone in Lori's eyes. "I'll tell you about it later. Have fun on your date." Lori moved away, and Norah pushed through the door just as her phone vibrated in her pocket.

Sterling had arrived at the car, wondering where she was. Instead of typing a response, she hurried into the parking lot, nearly going down on a patch of black ice.

"Sorry," she said. "I saw a friend and we got talking." She unlocked the car, but he didn't get in.

He stared at her feet before his eyes traveled to hers. "What's under the coat?"

"Wouldn't you like to know?" she teased as she moved around the car and sank into the driver's seat.

He got in and adjusted his injured leg. "Yes, I would." He reached for the hem of her coat, but she gently batted his hand away.

"You'll have to be patient."

He chuckled, this time without a trace of nerves, and the sound made the hair on the back of Norah's neck stand up in anticipation.

"You'll have to tell me where Migliano's is."

He directed her there, her fingers tightening on the steering wheel with every turn that brought them closer to the restaurant. She parked behind the building, a historic marker in Gold Valley that had been restored a decade ago.

Sterling waved away her help this time, but as soon as he'd found his balance, she tucked her hand into his elbow as much for his benefit as for hers.

He held the door open for her and stepped to the hostess. "I'm Sterling Maughan. I called about a reservation."

"Of course, Mister Maughan." She collected two menus. "Right this way."

Because she was trying to take everything in, Norah could hardly keep up with Sterling, and he moved at the speed of a snail. The ambiance of the restaurant screamed romance, from the low lamp light on each table, the cloth napkins, the tall champagne flutes. Saucy music played in the background, and the floor sported beige carpet with red roses woven through it.

If she'd had any doubts about this being a date, the décor of Migliano's would've eradicated them.

"Here you are." The hostess waited until both Norah and Sterling had sat, then she opened the menu for them.

"Thank you." Sterling flashed her a blinding smile, and she walked away. He focused on Norah. "Oh, dang. You forgot to take off your coat." His grin would've made the Cheshire Cat seem sane. He slid out of the booth. "Let me help you."

Norah swallowed and stood, unbuttoning her coat with frozen fingers. She shrugged out of the coat, Sterling's warm hands sliding over her shoulders as he took the jacket. His touch sent skitters down her back, and she shivered as attraction tiptoed through her.

Norah tugged on the bottom of the dress to get it to reach her knees, her skin as prickly as if she'd been doused with cold water.

But one look at Sterling's face, and all ideas about the cold thawed under the heat in his gaze.

He stepped into her personal space, his arm sliding around her waist like he'd done it countless times. Pressing a kiss to her cheek, he whispered, "Dang, Norah. You look great."

"Thank you." She gripped his elbows to keep herself upright as he lingered in the embrace.

"Okay." He cleared his throat. "That was worth the wait." Sterling released her, slid into the booth, and turned his attention to the menu.

Norah copied him, but not before she noticed the flush that had crawled up his neck and stained his cheeks. "What's good here?" she asked.

"The better question is what *isn't* good here?"

Norah set down her menu, embracing her daring side. The daring side of her that wore tight, black dresses with red heels. The daring side of her that went out with handsome men.

"Order something for me, then," she said, enjoying the kick of his mouth as he smiled and tried to hide it.

"You want me to order for you?"

Norah leaned her elbows on the table. "I think it'd be fun, don't you?"

CHAPTER 6

Sterling ordered the crab cakes as an appetizer, studied Norah for a few seconds to enjoy the shape of her mouth as he fumbled for what she'd like to drink. He finally came up with, "Diet Coke for her. I'll take Mountain Dew."

Norah ducked her head, her curls bouncing. Sterling wanted to touch her hair, find out if it felt as soft as it looked. "Of course," she murmured.

He focused on the waitress. "And I need a couple of minutes to order the rest."

"No problem. I'll get this appetizer in and bring your drinks."

Sterling focused on the menu as she walked away, his fantasies about holding and kissing Norah eradicating the words in front of him. He liked her—liked the way she looked and smelled and acted. He appreciated her, from the way she took care of him to the confessions about her taking care of her family. He wondered what sacrifices she'd made to be there at dinner with him.

But what would she like to eat? Images of bland soup and flat bread floated through his mind. Probably not something spicy, though the Italian fare didn't promise such things anyway.

Maybe lasagna. Chicken parmesan. Fettuccine Alfredo?

The waitress returned and Sterling still hadn't decided.

"You ready to order?"

He slapped his menu closed and met Norah's eye. She smirked at him, her hands folded over her already closed menu.

"Yeah," he said. "I'll take the beef and mushroom ravioli." He glanced at Norah and swallowed. "And she'll have the eggplant parmesan, with fettuccine Alfredo instead of spaghetti."

"It's a dollar extra to switch out the pasta."

Sterling waved his hand. "No problem."

Across from him, Norah stiffened, her intoxicating eyes dropping to the tabletop for a moment.

"Those crab cakes will be right out." The waitress collected their menus and left, leaving Sterling alone with Norah. He'd dreamt of this dinner for two straight days, but somehow now, he couldn't seem to get his voice to work.

"So you think you'll like working at Silver Creek?" Norah lifted her soda to her lips.

Sterling watched, mesmerized. When she caught him staring, heat flashed up his neck and into his face. He needed to get himself together, and fast. "Yeah, I think so."

He absently rubbed the back of his neck. "I'm worried about riding though. I can't even drive." The back of his throat felt sticky and he reached for his drink.

"You have a while." Norah smiled at him, her presence and attitude comforting. "The position doesn't open up for six more weeks."

"Yeah." Sterling reached across the table and covered her hand with his. "I'll ask the doctor about it when I go next week." He grinned at the blush staining her cheeks. She obviously liked him too. The feeling between them had been two-sided, Sterling was sure of that.

"So did I get your order right?"

She twisted her hand and slid her fingers into his. "Did you call my brother or something?"

Sterling chuckled. "No. I swear," he added as her mouth hardened into a disbelieving line. "I didn't. Call him right now and ask him."

A smile softened her lips, and Sterling couldn't tear his gaze from them. Could he kiss her tonight, after this date? He hated that she'd come to get him, that he couldn't take her home and walk her to her front door. A rush of inadequacy flowed through him, and he almost removed his hand from hers.

"I always substitute spaghetti for Alfredo," she said. "I mean, I've never been anywhere this nice." She glanced around, and Sterling finally recognized the emotion streaming from her eyes. Insecurity.

Her words about caring for her family, going to school at night, and cleaning cabins on the weekends haunted him.

Maybe he shouldn't have brought her to the nicest restaurant in town. Why hadn't he realized she wouldn't be comfortable here?

Sterling glanced around, wondering how to escape this situation. He glanced at Norah, who'd erased the emotion from her eyes. Helplessness cascaded through his core. "But you like eggplant parmesan?"

A glint entered her eyes. "One of my favorites."

Satisfaction sang through Sterling. "So you think I can be strong enough to ride in six weeks?"

"Ask the doctor," Norah said as the waitress arrived with a steaming plate of crab cakes. "And you can come down and work with the horses until you're ready to ride one." She turned her attention to the food. "Wow, you weren't kidding. This looks fantastic, and I don't even like seafood."

Sterling's heart dropped and leapt at the same time. He wanted Norah to like the food. He wanted to spend time with her. At the same time, he realized that the woman across from him didn't really fit his mother's idea of a wife.

He pushed the thought away. He'd never been overly concerned about fitting into his mother's mold, and he certainly wasn't going to start now—especially when the beautiful creature across from him soothed his soul so completely.

———

"It's not as strong as I would've hoped." Dr. Henshaw made a note on Sterling's chart while Rex thumbed through something on his phone. "You've been doing the physical therapy exercises I asked you to?"

Shame filled Sterling. "Well, I didn't really start until about a week and a half ago."

Dr. Henshaw exhaled as he set the folder down. "Well, that's why. Your leg will only get better if you use it."

Rex glanced up at the admonishing tone, his eyes sharp and probing.

Sterling looked at the scars on his leg. "Got it. I'll do them, I promise." The promise of riding at Silver Creek, of holding Norah's hand and strolling down the street, filled his mind.

"You're tolerating the pain okay?"

"It's manageable, as long as I don't miss my meds."

"I don't want you on such hard painkillers for much longer." Dr. Henshaw reached for his prescription pad. "Let's take you down to a high dose of ibuprofen and see if that's enough."

Sterling nodded, his stomach a tangled knot of nerves. He half-wished he hadn't asked Rex to come in with him. Drive him, sure. But he could've waited out in the front.

"So I have a question." Sterling barely squeezed the words out of his too-tight throat.

The doctor barely glanced up, finishing his signature with a flourish before focusing on Sterling.

"How long until I can do things? You know, climb the stairs, drive a car, ride a horse...."

Dr. Henshaw handed him the prescription, and Sterling almost crushed it in his fist. "You should be climbing stairs now. Get your leg back to its normal range of motion. Driving…let's wait on that another few weeks. I want you back in here in three, and if you're doing your therapy, I can probably clear you to drive then."

Relief slashed through Sterling. Only three more weeks. If he'd known how much the physical therapy mattered, he might not have neglected it so thoroughly. Even as he thought so, he knew he was wrong. It wasn't the physical pain that kept him from moving, from doing anything, from caring.

It was the mental anguish. The emotional turmoil.

He swallowed as Dr. Henshaw continued. "As for riding a horse, I suppose you can do that as long as the pain is tolerable. But I think it'll be too painful for a while. Too much movement."

"What about if it's just in a riding circle?" Sterling had cued up a few YouTube videos over the past few days. Introduction to riding, that sort of thing. Most people started on a slow horse, in a small circle. It hadn't looked too terribly difficult. Then again, Sterling was used to flying down mountains with a board strapped to both his feet.

"Do what feels right," Dr. Henshaw said. "It's your body. You need to listen to it. It'll tell you if you shouldn't be doing something." He touched Sterling's hip. "It's the hip I'm worried about with a horse. It might not be able to rotate that way yet."

The appointment concluded, and Sterling scheduled to come back in three weeks, his mind rotating around whether he should try riding right away, or just go to Silver Creek and learn general horse care, as Norah had suggested.

I'll call Owen, he decided as he left the office. He hadn't even buckled his seatbelt before Rex asked, "You want to ride a horse?"

Annoyance sang through Sterling. He didn't want to explain anything to his brother, though he had driven three hours round-trip just to get to the doctor's office. And he'd put in another three hours before he delivered Sterling at home and returned to his own house.

"Yeah," Sterling said. "I'm thinking about taking a job at Silver Creek." He wasn't just thinking about it. In his mind, the job was a done deal. A smile chased a way all the previous annoyance.

"Silver Creek?" Rex's disbelief screamed through the luxury car. "What's at Silver Creek?"

Sterling managed to put him off with an answer about combining his law enforcement education with something less dangerous, but really, it wasn't about *what* was at Silver Creek, but *who.*

———

Norah pulled into the garage at Six Sons Cabin, her nerves rioting against her. She wanted to be here. Wanted to take Sterling down to Silver Creek. Wanted to hold his hand, laugh with him, maybe kiss him at the conclusion of the afternoon.

She hadn't gotten her kiss after dinner last week. She'd

wanted it, and Sterling seemed like he did too, but the timing wasn't right. Both of them had felt it, because he'd told her to drop him off outside of the garage and he'd limped to the control panel to let himself in.

Norah had spent the next few hours lying in her dark bedroom, the feel of his hand in hers while the horror of bringing him home sliced through the fantasies of having a real relationship with him.

He hadn't asked about coming to her house again. Nor had he mentioned needing her to take him to movies or entertain him. In fact, they'd only texted a few times. Once, a long string that lasted hours as he told her about the doctor's visit. And again this morning as he asked her question after question about horseback riding.

She took a deep breath and squared her shoulders as she moved through the house to the spiral staircase that led to the basement. A delightful scent of antiseptic tinted with flowers met her nose, and the tidiness in the living room testified that Sterling had spent time cleaning up his space.

Ignoring the pill bottles on the counter, Norah grabbed a bottle of water from the fridge. "Sterling? You ready?"

"Coming!" His voice sounded from behind his closed bedroom door. She'd downed half the bottle of water before he emerged, and she instantly wished she hadn't.

The water sloshed against her stomach at the mere sight of him. Smelling like musky aftershave and minty toothpaste, he stood before her wearing a dark pair of jeans and a blue polo. A dark leather jacket covered most of that. His hair spiked in the front, glistening with gel or water, she wasn't sure.

No matter what, he made her throat dry up and her legs feel like sinking to the ground.

"Hey." He swept into her space, a joyous grin on his face. He put that strong arm around her waist and pressed a kiss to her temple. "You are a sight for sore eyes."

"How's your leg?" Norah regretted the question. She should've giggled and flirted back. Maybe told him how amazing he looked, and smelled, and would probably taste. She swallowed. "I mean, thanks. You look great too."

He chuckled, released her, and stepped toward the couch. "I just need my brace."

"Are you really going to try to ride today?"

"The doctor said I could as long as the pain was tolerable." He moved toward the kitchen. "Which reminds me…." He bypassed the orange bottles as he reached for a taller, white bottle. It still looked prescribed, and Sterling shook two pills into his palm before leaning over the kitchen faucet and swallowing them.

"Ready." He beamed at her, took her hand, and led her out the basement exit. The sidewalk had been cleared, and it took a sloping path up to the driveway.

"You shoveled?" she asked.

"Doc says I can do anything that doesn't cause pain." He squeezed her hand. "I'm trying to do more than watch Food Network."

She admired his strength. He seemed better than he had two weeks ago, but she also knew that sometimes looks were deceiving. That sometimes darkness crowded in when it was least expected. That sometimes it only took one wrong step to fall again.

"You learn how to make anything from those cooking shows?" she asked.

"Oh, yeah," he said. "Been experimenting and stuff."

She laughed, the sound free and full. She couldn't remember the last time she'd felt that way—or the last time she'd expressed it in front of someone. "Maybe you can cook me dinner."

He gained the top of the path, the ground leveling out. Sliding his arm around her shoulders, he drew her into his body. "I'd like that. When can you come?"

"Maybe tomorrow after church?" She watched him, trying to gauge his expression. The last time she'd invited him to church, he looked like she'd suggested he eat raw eggs followed by a shot of lemon juice. Then he'd scampered into his bedroom and closed the door with such finality, she wondered how long it had been since he'd gone to services.

"Church." His voice held a far away quality, and he moved into the garage with a glazed look in his eyes. "That's tomorrow, right?"

"Yes, it *is* Sunday tomorrow." Norah added a flirtatious smile to her teasing words as she extracted the keys from her pocket and unlocked the car. Why she thought she needed to secure her decade-old sedan inside the garage of a cabin that sat in a gated community, she wasn't sure.

Oh, but she was. She didn't dare leave her car unlocked

in her own garage. Her neighborhood didn't have gates, or long driveways, or the luxury of peace of mind. Such thoughts came at such random times, that Norah had a hard time reconciling them with her feelings about Sterling. When she was with him, everything felt right, like he would protect her and provide for her and love her. The look in his eyes and the softness of his touch spoke of that kind of relationship with him, the promise of an amazing future with him.

"What time is church?"

"Ten." She started the car and backed out of the garage. As soon as she pulled into the street, Sterling reached over and took her hand.

"You like going to church?" He asked in a genuine tone, a look of puzzlement on his strong brow.

"Yes," Norah said. "I like it. It's…." She exhaled, not quite sure how to sum up how she felt about attending church, about her relationship with God, in just a few words. She wasn't used to sharing personal things with people—even her few friends were more like acquaintances. She chanced a glance at Sterling and decided that she could trust him with this part of her life.

"It's an escape from Mama, number one."

His fingers on hers tightened for the briefest of breaths.

"I feel peaceful there," Norah added, her breath stuttering the tiniest bit as she inhaled. "Like things will work out and everything will be right in the end."

He allowed several beats of silence to pass before he said, "What's number two?"

Fear punctured her lungs, spread through her core. "I promised someone a long time ago that I'd make something of my life." She glanced at him to see if he could detect the slight untruth in her words. He didn't seem to, though his delicious, dark eyes drank her in. "Going to church helps me keep that promise."

She re-focused on the road so she wouldn't crash the car. Staring at him when he watched her with such intensity was definitely dangerous to her health.

"Who'd you promise?" he asked.

How he knew to ask the exact question she wished he wouldn't, how he knew to order her favorite foods, made her skin prickle.

She didn't want to tell him she'd made the promise to herself. That after she made it out of Silver Creek's treatment program, she needed something in her life to keep it on the straight and narrow. Her counselor, a forty-year-old woman with the most sarcastic sense of humor, had asked her to think about her life. In that rare moment of soberness, with Kathy looking seemingly into Norah's soul, Norah imagined what her life could be.

It had been eleven years, and Norah wasn't yet where she wanted to be. But she was working on it. And part of that included attending church and serving her neighbors.

"A friend of mine named Kathy," Norah said, so close to the edge of the truth it could've been the right answer. She hadn't said the words out loud to Kathy, but it was because of her counselor that Norah had decided to make something of her life, that she'd started going to church after her release from Silver Creek.

She pulled into the parking lot behind the stables and shifted her weight toward him. "So do you want to go tomorrow? We can get groceries after this, go to church in the morning, and you can demonstrate your new-found culinary skills tomorrow afternoon at the cabin."

The way he devoted his attention so fully to her made heat squirm through her veins, under her skin. She could practically see the wheels turning in his head. Finally, he said, "Sure, I can do that."

A grin burst across her face. A giddy grin, one she tried to wipe away before he saw it. But see it, he did. And he matched it with one of his own. A charge bolted between them, and Norah reached for the door handle before their first kiss happened in her beat-up car.

No, that wasn't where she'd first kiss Sterling. But she knew he wanted to kiss her, and the very thought made her lips tingle.

He straightened and strapped his leg brace on while she waited near the passenger door. "Here," he said, holding something toward her. "Gas money."

As quickly as her euphoria had flooded her, embarrassment chased it away. But she really couldn't afford to drive up to the cabins everyday, even if the craving to see Sterling called to her as loud as an air raid siren, so she took the money and moved to shove it in her pocket.

The number on the bill stunted her movement, stunned her into a statue. Sterling limped several paces away before

Norah could look away from the hundred-dollar bill. She hurried after him, anger slashing through her with the force of a Montana hailstorm.

She darted in front of him. "This is too much." She pressed the money against his chest.

He looked at her fingers on his body and then lifted his eyes to hers. Desire, and danger, and determination danced in their dark depths. "It's all I have." He moved to step around her.

"All you have is a hundred dollar bill?" She twisted and walked beside him. "I don't believe that. It's too much."

"Believe what you want. You're coming to get me everyday for the foreseeable future. I told you I'd pay for gas."

Norah shoved the money in her pocket and set her mouth in a tight line as he entered the stables and Owen greeted him. She couldn't have this conversation in mixed company. Wouldn't. So she glowered at the ease with which Sterling seemed to be able to do everything, despite his injury.

He brushed Blackjack, fed him, saddled him, and led him out to the walking circle. Norah followed along like a kicked puppy, the hundred-dollar bill burning a hole in her back pocket.

CHAPTER 7

Sunday morning, Norah found Javier perched at the kitchen counter, a bowl of oatmeal in front of him.

"I have to go pick up a friend. Save me two seats?" She flattened Javier's collar as he took a bite, his eyes trained on the sports highlight show. She still hadn't shown him the picture she'd snapped with Sterling, and adrenaline shot through her.

"Javier?" she asked as she moved into the kitchen to make hot chocolate. "You'll save me two seats, right?"

"Yeah, sure." He didn't look away from the TV.

"My friend is Sterling Maughan." Norah nonchalantly poured milk into a mug, noting the clang of silverware on their cheap formica. She opened the microwave and set her milk to heat for one minute before turning to face her brother.

"Sterling Maughan?" Javier's eyes looked wild, rabid almost.

Norah pulled out her phone and flicked to the picture she'd taken two weeks ago. "Yeah, I clean his family's cabin, and he was there, recovering after his injury." She showed Javier the picture. He clutched the phone, staring at the screen like he didn't believe the image to be real.

"He's coming to church with you?" Javier handed the phone back.

"Yeah." Norah turned when the microwave beeped and pulled her mug out. She added the hot chocolate mix and stirred. "We're going back to the cabin for lunch. Think you can handle making spaghetti for everyone?"

Javier's eyes narrowed. "Are you dating him or something?"

Norah choked and nearly spit out the mouthful of hot chocolate she'd taken. "No," she sputtered. "No, we're not…."

She couldn't even say the word *dating*. She wouldn't even think about that. So he'd held her hand a couple of times. Fine, *every* time they were alone together. He'd paid for dinner that one time, and he didn't know it, but he'd just bought Norah's family their groceries for the next week.

That didn't mean they were dating.

Her brain rioted against her heart, and Norah couldn't get anything involuntary to work. Her feet wouldn't move, though it was time to leave. Her hand wouldn't lift the hot chocolate to her mouth, though her thirst bordered on desperate.

Maybe you are dating Sterling Maughan, her brain said as it started to agree with the frantic pounding of her heart. That thought calmed her pulse, and she swung into motion. "Just save us two seats, okay?"

"Sterling Maughan is gonna sit by me at church," Javier said, his voice clouded with wonder.

Norah left her hot chocolate sitting on the counter. She wouldn't be able to drink it now anyway, not with the way her stomach tangoed with the possibility that she could be dating Sterling Maughan.

Church with Sterling felt like a science experiment, like everyone in Gold Valley had placed her and him under the microscope and couldn't stop adjusting the dials to get a closer look. Norah had given herself plenty of time to get up to the cabin and back, which meant they arrived early to the service.

A mistake, but not her first.

Oh no, that had come when she'd arrived at the cabin and found Sterling sitting at the dining room table on the main level of the house, decked out in his finest Sunday clothes. Norah wasn't sure what about a man in dark slacks, a white shirt, and a tie the color of rubies made her pulse pound, but seeing Sterling dressed up real nice certainly did the trick.

He stood—no leg brace—and smiled at her. He seemed genuinely happy to see her, and the squeeze in her fingers and the quick brush of his lips along her forehead spoke of that too.

She'd seriously underestimated what going to church with him would be like. Her thoughts had scattered upon seeing him, and she hadn't found them all yet. And now, the gossips of Gold Valley had zeroed in on the two of them together.

"You weren't lying." Javier arrived, which usually relieved Norah. "I totally thought you were lying!" He slid onto the bench next to Sterling. "You're Sterling Maughan. I just can't believe it. I didn't know you lived here."

Sterling's grip on Norah's fingers increased, but she slipped hers away. She'd told her brother she wasn't dating Sterling, and Javier hadn't seen them holding hands yet. "Sterling, this is my brother, Javier. Remember I told you he was a big fan?"

Sterling's jaw relaxed and he started talking to Javier like they were old friends. Their conversation allowed Norah to squeeze a few more inches between them, especially once Alex and Erik arrived, tumbling and talking, at their bench.

"Shh," Norah admonished as she waved them closer to her. "Stay here by me."

"I want to sit by Javvy," Erik complained. "He brought candy."

"Go around," Norah said. "My friend has a hurt leg. You can't climb over him."

Erik scrambled down the bench and around the back. His presence on that end of the pew pushed Sterling closer to Norah. He didn't seem to mind. In fact, he lifted his arm and rested it on the back of the bench behind her.

Javier definitely saw that, and Norah pressed her eyes closed, praying for a miracle. Praying that church would start already. Praying to know if she was indeed, dating Sterling Maughan.

"Good morning, brothers and sisters." The pastor stood at the front of the chapel, the microphone loud enough to cover the dwindling whispers. Relief sagged Norah's muscles—at least until Sterling's leg pressed against hers. She tensed, but she couldn't get any tighter than she already was. He sat ramrod straight, his fingers in fists, as the pastor spoke about seeing yourself the way the Lord sees you.

Norah had heard this particular sermon before, and she still struggled to do what the pastor advised. She couldn't see herself the way God did. She didn't see herself as lovable, or worthy of forgiveness, though she did feel loved by God, and forgiven for the things she'd done wrong.

She listened intently, hoping to hear something different this time she hadn't last time—and to keep herself from obsessing over why the sermon seemed to bother Sterling so much.

Sitting in church, Sterling felt every bit as uncomfortable as he thought he would, like he'd been caught cheating on a crucial exam and everyone could see it. Everyone seemed to be looking at him, and the way Norah's brother exclaimed his name, everyone in Gold Valley would know he was in town by nightfall.

He shouldn't care. His family was well-known in Gold Valley, and he wasn't here to hide. At least not anymore.

He forced himself to uncurl his fists, then he reached for Norah's hand. She gave it to him a bit grudgingly, but he needed the anchor she provided. The pastor spoke of loving and forgiving yourself, the way God did.

At first, his words caused a sting of anger to prick Sterling's mind. God didn't love him. If He did, He certainly hadn't shown it that day on the mountain.

But Sterling did believe that God forgave people. That truth sang softly to him, slowly easing the tension in Sterling's body. When the closing hymn began, the nerves returned. Could he duck out now?

He glanced at Javier, and his plans to wait for Norah in the car vanished. He couldn't get past the guy with his injured leg without causing a scene. So he sat rigid and still, hoping people would mind their own business until he could escape. He even found himself praying for such a miracle.

Song, and prayer, and church ended. Sterling hadn't been to church in at least five years, and he'd survived his first time back. He took his first full breath in an hour and stood to test the weight on his leg. When it held, he followed Javier out of the chapel as fast as his limp would allow him, Norah's hand still secured in his.

"See you at home," Norah said to Javier. She released Sterling's hand to bend down and give her other two brothers quick hugs. "You listen to Javvy. Don't bother Mama."

They nodded, their dark eyes solemn and serious.

"I'll be back tonight." She looked at Sterling, who took that as an invitation to leave the church. Outside, the wind howled as it brought in another storm. He ducked lower into his jacket to ward off the icy claws of the air as it tried to tickle his spine. He'd never been so thankful for a Montana storm in his life, but this one ensured no one would be stopping in the parking lot to chat. Everyone who'd exited before them bent into the wind, their collars high and their gloved hands gripping their coats closed.

Norah unlocked the car from ten feet away, and they spilled into the relative safety of the sedan. She started it and cranked the heat, though it would take a few minutes for the air to actually get warm.

"So you survived," she said as she backed out.

"I actually thought that when the service ended." He chuckled. "And it wasn't that bad. That pastor actually said some good things."

Norah cocked an eyebrow at him. "You think he said good things?"

"Yeah, didn't you?"

"That's actually a recycled sermon," she said. "I've heard it before, and yes, it's good. You just seemed…."

He waited for her to continue, interested in what she thought of him. In fact, he realized as she drove, that her opinion was the *only* one he cared about. Let the townspeople talk. Let them speculate why he was at the cabin, how long he'd stay, and what Norah meant to him.

He didn't care.

He only cared what *she* thought.

"I seemed what?" he asked when she remained silent.

"Tense."

Oh, he'd been tense all right. "I haven't been to church in a long time, Norah." His voice came out hushed, almost embarrassed, though he didn't feel that way.

"First time for everything," she said, either ignoring or not hearing the clumsily veiled emotion in his words.

"Is that why you bought jicama yesterday?"

She giggled, and the sound lit every nerve in his body. "It's a great vegetable," she said. "I emailed you that slaw recipe. Did you get it?" She glanced at him with an edge of concern in her expression he found adorable. No, sexy.

"I got it."

"You should have the knife skills by now, considering how much television you watch." She grinned at him, and his heart banged against his ribs. He reached for her hand, pleased when she let him take it easily this time. He brought her knuckles to his lips, wondering—not for the first time— what it would be like to kiss Norah Watson.

———

It turned out that actually using a knife and understanding how to use a knife were two totally different things. Sterling couldn't make matchsticks out of carrots and jicama any more than he could rewind time and prevent himself from falling down a mountain and breaking his leg.

Norah seemed annoyingly amused by the whole thing. "You promised me a gourmet lunch," she said when he huffed in frustration and tossed the knife into the sink. He cringed at the resulting clanging of metal on metal. "Don't tell my mom I did that." He glanced in the sink but didn't see any marks. "How about we order pizza? At Berlio's, they have gourmet items."

Norah rolled her eyes as Sterling limped around the counter and sat next to her on a barstool. "No, look." He swiped and tapped and pulled up the menu. "It even says 'gourmet' right in the title."

She glanced at the phone, her dark eyes sparkling like diamonds. When her eyes met his, they hooked, held, harbored secrets he wanted to take careful seconds to unwrap. She leaned closer to him, and the tether that had drawn him to her from the moment he saw her dancing in the kitchen upstairs crackled with electricity.

He could kiss her now. Right now. She wouldn't say no. He wanted to.

He leaned closer too, their breath mingling together. His hand migrated to her elbow, slid up her arm.

Her phone went off at the same time someone rang the doorbell. She jerked away from him, the barstool she'd been sitting on scraping across the tile floor. "It's my brother," she said. "Can you get the door?"

It would take him at least five minutes to get up the stairs, especially because he'd abandoned the brace that morning when he realized it wouldn't fit under his father's slacks.

"Sure," he said anyway. Hopefully whoever had decided to make a house call would leave before he could get to the door.

Sterling cursed the architect, the designer, and the construction crew that had built the spiral staircase leading to the main floor. Steps shouldn't be so narrow and steep. He hobbled through the living room and past the kitchen to the official front door. He paused with his hand on the knob, sending a rushed prayer heavenward that he'd taken too long to get there.

Relief rushed his body when he opened the door and found only empty space. Well, and a loaf of banana bread. He stooped for it, looked left and right again, and closed the door. Seizing an opportunity, he punched the "call" button on the pizza website he'd brought up earlier. It wasn't exactly the opportunity he wanted to take with both hands, and his thoughts drifted to how Norah's lips might taste, how her slender fingers would feel sliding through his hair, how he could get drunk on her from only her perfume.

With two gourmet pizzas on the way, he descended back to the basement, where he found the subject of his fantasies curled into the corner of the sectional couch. "Everything okay at home?" he asked.

"Yeah, Javier just wanted to know if they could rent a movie."

Sterling catalogued that her brother—who had to be close to an adult—called Norah to get approval for something as simple as renting a movie. Norah, not their mother. To rent a movie.

The woman had more layers to her life than Sterling knew. But he wanted to peel them back one by one, experience her life and share it with her. The thought scared him as much as it excited him.

"What movie do they want?" he asked.

"I don't know." She reached for a blanket and covered her legs. "Sorry about Javier at church. I told him you'd be there, but I forgot to warn him not to act like a crazed fan."

Sterling shrugged, though he hadn't enjoyed the spotlight as much as he once had. "It's okay."

"He's watched every one of your interviews. Every run that was broadcast."

He squirmed. "Is that why you knew who I was?" He sat next to her on the couch, close enough to be friendly, but not close enough to kiss. Unfortunately.

"Yeah. I used to stay up with him until—"

"Until what?"

She shrugged her arms under the blanket, and Sterling had the distinct impression that she was using it as a shield. "Until Mama went to bed. Then we could watch what he wanted without her getting upset."

The desire to hold her, smooth away the rough parts of her life, spiked. "I'm sorry about your mom."

"Me too." She inhaled sharply and caught his eyes. "I mean—"

"I know what you mean." The moment between them stretched, solidified. "My mom is no picnic either."

"Your mom's great."

Sterling really shouldn't complain, though his list of flaws for his mother was obviously longer than Norah's. "You're right," he said. "She's great."

Norah studied him, and he didn't like the way she cocked her head. Loud knocking sounded on the door through the kitchen and around the corner, and he practically leapt up to answer it.

"Who's that?" she asked as he walked away.

"We've had a slight change in the menu." He tossed her a smile as he went to get the pizzas, grateful the delivery driver had followed his instructions and brought the order to the basement entrance.

An hour later, fully satiated with cheese and meat, as well as more root beer than a human should be allowed to consume, Sterling placed the Blu-ray disc in the player and collapsed on the couch.

"Cooking is hard work," he complained as he lined up the remote controls next to him.

"You ordered pizza." Norah had seemed to enjoy the gourmet pizzas as much as he'd told her she would. She ate the side salad he'd bought, and two of the garlic breadsticks.

"That slaw wore me out. I have no idea what shape I'd be in if I'd attempted to make those pork chops." He leaned back into the couch and put his feet on the ottoman. "You should take them home with you. Javier seems like a real meat-eater."

She tossed her curls and laughed. "He does love a good piece of meat. Not as much as pizza, though."

"Well, I'm glad he has his priorities straight." Sterling hated the distance between them, wanted her right next to him on the couch so he could hold her hand, or put his arm around her, or kiss her if they somehow looked at each other with the need they had earlier.

"You gonna sit all the way over there all day?" He could barely believe he'd spoken. Fire raced to his face, and he almost coughed to punctuate his flapping tongue.

"Where do you want me to sit?" Her flirtatious tone nearly undid Sterling's composure. The composure he'd been trying to keep since seeing her walk through his door wearing a black skirt with a bow on the waist and a red and white polka dot top that hugged every line of her body.

"Right here," he said, indicating the seat cushion beside him. "Next to me."

"Well…." She made no move to scoot closer.

"I went to church this morning," he said. "The least you can do is sit by me to soothe my wounded soul."

She scoffed, then giggled, then slid over, coming close enough to snuggle into his side. She lifted the blanket over both of their legs, careful not to jostle his injury. He took the deepest breath he could manage, almost tasting the strawberry and rose of her hair. He sighed, more content with Norah than he'd been with anyone in years. Even more content than he'd been after winning the gold medal.

Sure, he'd been happy then. Excited. Overjoyed. But he wouldn't say he was content.

He leaned his head back, enjoying the feeling of holding

Norah in his arms and breathing in the creamy quality of her skin.

Several minutes later—or an hour—or maybe only seconds had passed—Norah hissed his name. He let the musical sound of her voice float in his mind, though he knew he should open his eyes.

"Sterling," she said again, louder now, drawing him out of the doze he'd fallen into.

He opened his eyes and blinked, trying to make the room come into focus, to remember the last thing he'd been doing.

Holding Norah.

He still did, though she'd straightened a bit and felt stiff next to him.

"Well," a man said, causing Sterling's heart to hammer and his neck to crane to see behind him.

Rex stood there, his arms folded, the elbows of his designer suit taut. "This looks comfortable."

CHAPTER 8

Sterling scrambled to his feet, leaving Norah in a folded ball on the couch. He retreated away from her, the spot where he'd been cold. Her heart shriveled under the scrutiny of Rex Maughan, the man who ran the family's real estate empire. Norah had been cleaning the cabin long enough to know who he was.

Rex, of course, had no idea who she was. At least she didn't think he did. But then she heard him hiss, "You can't be cuddling up to the help," and all the air went out of her lungs.

The help.

Was that all she'd ever be?

Sterling pushed his brother further down the hall and around the kitchen, one fist curled and his eyes shooting her an apologetic look over his shoulder before he disappeared. Still, her insides quaked like someone had set them in gelatin and then shook her.

Angry snippets of conversation wafted back to her, and she wondered if either man knew the kitchen walls didn't actually connect to the ceiling. Norah knew. She dusted up there every week. Or rather, she had every week except for the last two. Sterling had steadfastly refused to let her downstairs to clean, claiming he could do it himself. But surely he wasn't dusting.

Norah stood on numb legs, her mind whirring as fast as a fan set on high. She didn't remember telling herself to put on her shoes, or collect her purse, or fumble for her keys. Somehow she made it up the spiral stairs without falling to her death. The cold finally shocked her out of her stupor, and she realized she'd gotten in her car and was gripping the steering wheel.

"Just go," she whispered while at the same time her heart begged her to stay. Even though she'd moved like she was underwater, Sterling wouldn't have a chance of catching her if she wanted to leave.

But do you want to leave?

Of course she didn't. Before Rex's Italian loafers had woken her, she'd been dreaming of a kiss with Sterling, right there in the basement where they'd spent that stormy night together. Nowhere else would do in Norah's mind.

Now, though, the basement held angry words, and awkward conversations, and so much tension it made Norah's teeth clench.

Someone knocked on the window, and she yelped and startled toward the middle of the car. Sterling's face took her breath away, which didn't combine well with the thrumming of her heart and the adrenaline coursing through her.

He made a motion for her to roll down the window, but she hadn't actually put the key in the ignition yet. She opened the door instead, still mostly numb—at least from the ears down.

"Norah, don't go." Sterling stepped back while she got out of the car, and he held his arms bolted across his chest, which only enhanced the size of his biceps.

"Come back inside." He gazed at her evenly, making her heart crack. But she couldn't be put back together with metal rods and physical therapy.

"It's cold out here," he said.

"It's not that warm in there."

Sterling flinched. "He left."

"I should go anyway."

He took a stunted step forward, fell back. "Please come back inside."

She couldn't ignore the desperation in his voice, the frantic edge in his eyes. She both wanted to follow him back to the basement and jump in her car and never return to Six Sons Cabin.

Of course, she couldn't do that. Nancy Maughan paid too well to do a little dusting and a lot of vacuuming. Norah hated the siren call of money—just as much as she adored the way Sterling's gaze clung to her, sucked her in, devoured her.

"Okay." She sighed.

He smiled, but the action came and went so fast Norah

barely saw it. "Okay." He ushered her in front of him, allowed her to help him down the spiral staircase though his step was much more sure now. He kept his hand on her shoulder after they reached the basement and deftly slid it down her arm to her hand.

"I'm sorry, Norah." His voice sounded like deep, dark, melting chocolate. Smooth and rich and utterly irresistible. Norah closed her eyes and savored the way her name sounded against his tongue.

"Tell me more about your brothers," she said as she settled back into her previous spot on the couch, the movie long forgotten.

Sterling sat next to her, and the disgruntled look on his face could've come from a flash of pain from his leg as he lifted it to rest on the ottoman, or it could've been because of her request.

"If you tell me about yours," he countered with a mischievous glint in his eyes.

A blip of fear made her heart skip a beat. But if she was interested in spending more time with him—and she was— he'd find everything out eventually. Too bad the very idea of him ever seeing where and how she lived caused lightning to strike her bloodstream.

She took a deep breath to summon that brave woman who wore little black dresses and let gorgeous men order her meal. "Okay. You first."

———

Sterling didn't know where to start when it came to his family. Being the youngest had always been hard, especially with five perfect older brothers.

"Henry is my favorite," he started. "He lives in Washington D.C."

"He's the lawyer." Norah leaned her head against the back of the couch, tilting her head at just the right angle to expose her slender neck.

Sterling licked his lips and tried to reign in his thoughts. After what Rex had said, any hope of kissing Norah had fled. Sterling had pushed his leg farther than he thought possible when he'd discovered her gone. He paused, remembering his pleas to the Lord to let her be in the garage. And she had been. And she'd come back inside.

Thank you, he thought.

"Yeah, he's the lawyer," he said out loud. "And surprisingly, he's not the stuffiest of my brothers. His wife is a marathon runner, and they have three kids."

"Why's he your favorite?"

Sterling shrugged, though he knew exactly why. He just didn't want to voice his insecurities out loud.

"Who's your favorite?" he asked instead.

"Javier," she answered without hesitation. "I was ten when he was born, and he was the cutest little baby." A fond smile spread her lips, and Sterling reached out and tucked her hair behind her ear.

Their eyes locked, and the sizzling heat between them hadn't dimmed despite Rex's insensitive words.

"Henry's my favorite because he told me once he wanted

to be a police officer." Sterling's voice sounded tight and haunted, but he didn't know how to normalize it. "He said he was proud of me for doing what I wanted to do, and not conforming to Mom's ideals." Sterling swallowed, suddenly needing a drink to water the desert his throat had become. "Said he wished he'd been brave enough to do that when he was younger."

Norah's natural beauty shone in her face as she allowed herself to relax. "What did your mother want you to be?"

"You know, a banker like my brother Elliot, or a surgeon like my brother Andrew. Henry and Nathan went into law. Rex runs my dad's real estate firm. Something like that, with letters after my name."

"You have a title." She smiled, the gesture pinning her onto Sterling's heart. "Officer Maughan, GVPD. Very authoritative. Regal, almost."

He chuckled. "Right. Regal. That's me." He sobered and laid his cheek on the back of the couch too. Facing Norah, watching her blink and breathe and just be, a perfect sense of comfort threaded through him.

"I'm really sorry about what Rex said."

Her eyes turned glassy. "I don't want to talk about it."

"I don't think you're the help."

She took a deep breath. "I do clean your house."

"It's not my house."

"You're living here right now, and your mother pays me."

His lungs tightened. "You're right. I don't want to talk about this." He straightened, wishing Rex had just stayed in Missoula. His brother had claimed he wanted to see how

Sterling was doing—and Sterling didn't doubt that. He just wished he'd called or something beforehand.

Would it have mattered? he asked himself.

And he hated that the answer was yes. Sterling wouldn't have invited Norah over after church—he wouldn't have even gone to church that morning—and he wouldn't have put on a romantic comedy, cuddled up to Norah, and fallen asleep.

"Tell me more about the center." He was officially starting his job at Silver Creek the next morning. He wouldn't be working with a group of boys for a few more weeks, until the cycle ended and a new one began. But he'd become familiar with the horses and shadow the at-risk group to see how they operated.

As Norah started telling him about the equine therapy program and the role of counselors like her, he realized she hadn't said much about her brothers. Part of him wished he'd asked about them instead of the center, but another part just liked hearing the sound of her voice, no matter what she said.

———

The next morning, Sterling's stomach swooped as Norah pulled into the staff parking lot on the north end of the Silver Creek property. "It's a bit of a hike to the front office," she said. "But you can stop at the stables, talk to Owen, see the horses."

He nodded, the thought of the animals comforting him.

He hadn't thought much about horses or therapy, but from his limited encounter with Blackjack over the weekend, he found them soothing.

Norah stayed by his side, and as much as he wanted to reach for her hand and draw from her strength, he didn't. The winter morning probably had something to do with why he kept his hands in his pockets. Or maybe he was still unsettled from how things had gone the previous day. She'd left before dinnertime, claiming her family needed her at home, and Sterling had spent hours in front of the television, brooding.

Rex had texted and then called, and Sterling ignored him. Juvenile, maybe, but his brother had really put a kink in his budding relationship with Norah, and Sterling found he didn't have anything nice to say.

His mother always said not to say anything in those situations. This morning, right as Norah arrived, Sterling had texted Rex. Just a couple of words. *Call you tonight.* He still didn't know what to say, but at least he didn't feel like smashing something anymore.

He entered the stable to find several teenage boys feeding the horses. They looked at him and Norah, and Sterling was supremely glad he wasn't holding her hand. Owen moved down the aisle, giving instructions. Another man stood near the end of the barn. Sterling couldn't see his features, only his outline against the bright morning light.

"That's Will," she said. "He's their counselor. So he makes sure the boys are up, and here on time, and that they listen to Owen and do a good job. Then he'll take them to breakfast."

"So that's what you do? What I'll be doing?" Sterling stepped up to a dark brown horse that had been fed already. The horse lifted its head and Sterling ran his hand along its cheek, stealing the much-needed calmness from the animal instead of Norah.

"Right."

"Do counselors live on-site?" he asked. "What if the kids need something in the middle of the night?"

"There's a night staff," Norah said. "I've only been called in a couple of times during an emergency. It's not bad."

As Sterling continued through the stable, past a barn, and between rows of a half-dozen buildings, that same peaceful feeling that had permeated his soul last Saturday descended again. He probably should've asked more questions, been better prepared to start a job where a teen's life was involved. But he felt so right about being at Silver Creek, the unknowns weren't that important.

Norah entered the office building ahead of him and introduced him to the staff. A secretary named Shelly handed him a folder. "He'll want you to sign all of that in front of him. He's waiting for you."

Sterling didn't expect Norah to come into Dr. Richards' office with him, but she did. And she closed the door behind her. A red flag lifted in Sterling's mind. He glanced at Norah, but she shrugged one shoulder. She tapped something out on her phone, and his buzzed as he handed Dr. Richards the folder.

"Just set it there, yes." Dr. Richards didn't look away from his computer. "Just give me one minute…."

Sterling checked his phone. *He asked me to come in with you. I don't know why.*

When? Sterling sent back.

Got a text from him this morning. Sorry, I forgot to tell you.

Sterling glanced at her, hoping his expression said, *It's okay,* because Dr. Richards exhaled and leaned away from his computer and he couldn't text. "So how are you guys this morning?"

"Great," Sterling said. Norah said nothing, her face stoic and unreadable.

Dr. Richards flipped open the folder. "So for the next month, you'll be working with Will. He's the counselor that will be leaving. He'll orient you to the facilities, the schedule, that kind of thing." He slid a paper toward Sterling. "I need you to sign this. It says you won't discuss the patient's cases outside of the staff at Silver Creek."

Sterling picked up a pen and put his signature on the page. He repeated it for several more as Dr. Richards told him he'd be working with Owen twice a week, as the at-risk boys generally benefitted the most from equine care and therapy.

"You'll also be taking a Love and Logic course," Dr. Richards said. "We've already paid for you and enrolled you in the course we host here. It's on Thursday evenings."

Sterling signed the enrollment paper, and Dr. Richards closed the folder. Confusion needled his mind. Why was Norah here?

Dr. Richards looked at her, and then back to Sterling. "I understand you two have been spending a lot of time together."

Sterling fell back in his chair like he'd been punched, but Norah leaned forward. "What do you mean?" she asked.

"You went to dinner after the orientation. Someone said they saw you sitting together at church."

Sterling's eyebrows drew down. "She's giving me a ride down here each day too." He tapped his leg brace. "I haven't been cleared to drive yet."

"So you're friends." Dr. Richards somehow managed to watch both of them at the same time, and Sterling didn't like the scrutiny.

He looked at Norah, slightly horrified. He definitely wanted to be more than friends with her. She blinked at him, clearly not expecting this conversation either.

"Yeah," he finally said. "We're friends."

"Friends is fine." Dr. Richards leaned forward, his face stern and serious. "Anything more than friends is against our policy here at Silver Creek."

Norah started laughing, and Sterling couldn't tell if it was maniacal or forced. Maybe both. "Don't worry about that," she told Dr. Richards, steadfastly keeping her gaze away from Sterling. "I clean Sterling's family's cabin." She finally pinned him with a pointed look that stabbed, stabbed, stabbed right through his heart. "Our relationship is strictly professional."

"I'm glad to hear that." Dr. Richards stood. "Well, Norah,

I'm sure your girls are expecting you. And Sterling, Owen's ready to show you the ins and outs of horse care."

His words echoed in Sterling's ears, combining with the damaging ones Norah had spoken.

I clean Sterling's cabin-bin-bin.

Our relationship is strictly professional-nal-nal.

He stood, his injured leg feeling like wood, and hobbled out of the office, wondering if Norah had spoken true or if she'd just said those things to appease Dr. Richards and his policy.

Either way, the pain in his chest continued to throb, and thrum, and torture him for the rest of the day.

He couldn't date Norah if they worked at Silver Creek together?

Sterling suddenly didn't want the job that had felt so right and so perfect. Didn't want it at all.

CHAPTER 9

Norah survived the day after the blindsiding meeting in Dr. Richards office. Not much more could be said for the hours she spent at Silver Creek. Part of her still existed in shock over Dr. Richards's policy and his questions about her and Sterling's relationship. Who had told him they'd gone to dinner after the orientation? Or to church together? And how was that any of his—or anyone's—business?

Anger accompanied her through her tasks, keeping her mind sharp and her hands quick as she worked. By the time she met Sterling in the barn, she felt one breath away from snapping.

He didn't step forward to greet her, didn't sweep his arm around her waist, didn't brush his lips along her forehead the way he had several times before. The loss of the affection stung, and the hurt spiraled deeper that Norah knew it could. After all, she hadn't been interested in dating, or men, or marriage, ever. But Sterling had changed that, made her wonder if she was loveable, if she could have a future and a family with someone besides Mama.

"Hey." She stopped a healthy distance from him, her hands stuffed in her jeans pockets.

He looked at her with exhaustion in the set of his jaw. "Hey."

She didn't want to let go of the hope that had ballooned at the prospect of a relationship with him. She suspected that would hurt worse than anything else she'd endured in her life. "You ready to get home?"

"I'm so tired," he said. "I'm not sure I can even walk to the car." He flashed her a faint smile but didn't seem to have the energy to keep it on his face for longer than a moment. "Who knew riding a horse could take so much out of a person?"

Norah could sympathize, so she gave him her best grin. "Well, come on. You can tell me where to stop for dinner on the way."

"Thanks. I'm starving." He did move much slower than he had that morning, and she caught him wincing a couple of times as he stepped on his injured leg.

"Did you take your meds today?" she asked.

"I forgot to bring them." Sterling leaned against the car and panted. "I asked for some ibuprofen at the office at lunchtime. I'll be okay." He ducked down into the car.

She kept both hands on the wheel, unsure of which

spying eyes she needed to avoid. He directed her through a drive-through Chinese restaurant, and she maneuvered up the mountain while he ate an egg roll.

She pulled into the garage and carried the food bags inside while he closed the garage door. He locked the entrance to the house too, and didn't flick on any lights as he came nearer to her in the kitchen.

His pinky brushed hers. "I can't believe that policy." His voice sounded like a warm summer breeze, and it tickled the back of her neck. His hand settled fully into hers, and her heart danced in her chest.

His other arm swept around her and pulled her close. Those delicious lips traced themselves across her eyebrows. "I don't want to just be friends," he whispered next.

"But we need you at the center for the at-risk boys." She matched her tone to his in volume and pitch. She wanted to stomp on the accelerator of their relationship at the same time she applied pressure to the brakes.

"I'm not gonna quit." But he didn't let her go either.

"Then what—?"

"We'll just have to be more discreet." He stepped back and pulled out a couple of Chinese food containers. "Why is there a policy like that, anyway?"

"I thought it was for the patients," Norah said. "You know, we don't want our boys and girls getting mixed up with each other. They come from all over the country, and they're not at Silver Creek to find a date."

Sterling nodded as he opened the cupboard and got out

two plates. "But for the adults there? Seems sort of…old-fashioned."

"I didn't know." Norah spooned beef and broccoli onto her plate and added a scoop of ham-fried rice.

"You did a great job convincing Dr. Richards we were just friends." Sterling's tone possessed an edge of something dangerous.

"We are friends."

"Norah."

"I do clean your cabin."

"It's *not* my cabin."

She looked up from her food to find his gaze set on angry. "I know."

He deflated and added more Mongolian chicken to his pile of food. They ate in silence for a few minutes before Sterling dropped his fork to his plate. "I don't care about what my brother said. I don't care if no one approves of our relationship." He took a heaving breath that expanded his chest to nearly double its size. "I've always been the black sheep of the family, and I just don't care."

Norah wasn't quite sure what he wanted her to say in response. A sliver of joy pulsed through her, infecting her lips, and they twitched into a smile.

"Okay?" he asked. "Are we okay, then?"

"I'm okay." Norah believed the words, happiness spreading through her because she did. She truly believed she was okay, that she and Sterling could have a future despite his brother's statement.

"Good." Sterling reached over and took his hand in hers. "If you're okay, then I'm okay."

Norah prepared to leave as soon as she finished eating, telling Sterling, "I have to get home for my brothers. They rely on me to make dinner."

"Take the leftovers." Sterling started closing the containers and putting them back in the plastic bags. "Then you don't have to cook."

Relief swept through Norah, but she didn't let him see it. She had at least an hour of homework to finish tonight before her class tomorrow night, and a twenty-minute drive to the wrong side of the tracks.

Her newfound hope and joy withered under the remembrance of who she was. She ducked her head and headed for the garage, the leftover Chinese food in her hand. Sterling followed, reaching one of his long arms over her shoulder and pressing his palm against the door so she couldn't open it.

"You sure you're okay?"

She turned to face him, her pulse tap dancing against her ribs at his nearness, the scent of his skin. Seizing her bravery, she leaned into him, watched his eyes drift closed as he took a deep breath, and brushed her lips across his cheek. "I'm okay, Sterling. See you in the morning."

She opened the door and flew down the steps to her car while he opened the garage door. While it wasn't exactly the kiss she wanted to give him, it was all she had right now—especially after consuming so much spicy Chinese food.

A giddy grin accompanied her down the mountain and

all the way to her house, where she sat in the driveway and looked at the lone bulb lighting the front window. She felt physical weight descend on her as she got out of the car and entered the house.

"Chinese food," she announced as she placed the bag on the table. Javier jumped up from his place on the couch, Erik hot on his heels. Alex continued reading his book for a few seconds, then he set it aside and came into the kitchen.

"Well, it's about time you made it home." Mama's voice froze Norah's motion of opening the leftover sweet and sour chicken.

"She's not that late," Javier said, exchanging a look with Norah that said Mama was in one of her moods. She rarely came out of her bedroom while the family was still awake. Norah hadn't expected to see her until ten, her usual dinnertime.

"I'll make you a plate." Norah got out four plates and started putting rice and chicken onto one for her mom.

"How did you pay for this?" Mama's poisonous voice had rendered everyone silent. Norah nodded at them, and Javier understood. He hurried the younger boys to load their plates, and then they disappeared down the hall to his bedroom, where they could eat in peace.

Norah waited until the snick of the door closing reached her ears. "I didn't pay for it, Mama. A friend and I stopped to eat, and these are the leftovers." She made no move to sit down and share the meal with her mother. "I have home-work, so—"

"Who's your friend?" Mama settled at the table with her plate, the message for Norah to sit down just as clear.

"Just someone who started at the center." Norah perched on a barstool, not fully committing to staying. Everything about this situation had her on edge, as if Mama somehow knew about Sterling.

Maybe she did. After all, Dr. Richards did.

Pure panic iced Norah's insides, making her stomach tumble and twist and her heart pinch and pulse. "How are you feeling today, Mama?"

That seemed to derail her mother for a moment. She coughed until Norah felt sure she'd spit up blood, continued eating, and then said, "I've had better days."

"You have?" The question exploded out of Norah before she could censor it. She'd been spending too much time with Sterling, revealing too many things she'd kept bottled up for so long, she'd lost her ability to suppress her tongue.

"Yes." Her mother looked at her sharply. "But not when you were born, or any of those boys. That's for sure." She stabbed a piece of chicken and stuck it in her mouth. Norah had heard her say such hurtful things before, but they still dug against Norah's heart, stabbing in her brain.

She stared evenly back at her mother, her throat swollen, as she thought about the stark contrast between her home and Sterling's. The feeling that prevailed at the cabin spoke of love, while here, all Norah sensed was fear. Even if Sterling wasn't happy with his parents, or felt like they didn't accept him, he knew they loved him. Norah marveled at that, and wondered what it would be like to be loved so unconditionally.

God loves you unconditionally. The pastor's words entered her mind at that moment, eradicating some of the fear, and completely silencing her mother's next words. Norah managed to nod, then she stood and moved down the hall to her bedroom.

She didn't want to be infected with more of her mother's lies. Before entering her room, she knocked lightly on Javier's door and then opened it. All three boys sat on his bed, their food gone, as a movie played on his cheap laptop.

Closing the door behind her, she released the love she felt for her three half-brothers. *They should know someone loves them,* she thought. Without a word, she moved across the room and hugged her brothers. "I love you guys," she whispered, saddened and also joyous that all three of her brothers—including the almost eighteen-year-old Javier—clung to her and gave her the sentiment in return.

Before she could cry, she straightened. "Okay, guys," she said. "I have to finish my homework. Finish the movie, and then it's time for bed."

"Can we sleep in here?" Alex asked Javier.

"Sure thing." Javier stacked the plates and handed them to Norah. She closed his door behind her and faced the kitchen. She couldn't hear anything, and she'd normally avoid another altercation with her mother. But, feeling stronger and braver than she ever had, she walked into the kitchen, prepared for whatever happened.

Mama was gone. She'd left her half-eaten plate of food

on the table for Norah to clean up. In a rare act of defiance, Norah put away the leftovers, loaded the dishwasher with her brother's plates—but left her mother's—before pulling her backpack from the front closet and settling onto the couch to finish her homework.

Sterling endured the week, though it felt like the closest thing to torture he'd experienced—besides the actual fall. But it took so much energy to keep things cool between him and Norah at work. So much physical power to keep himself on the horse, or following around eight teenage boys and their surly counselor.

Norah had class on Tuesday and Thursday nights, and barely had time to run him home before she drove to the small campus on the eastern edge of town. Sterling missed her all day, and not being able to share dinner with her racked his soul as he had to spend his evenings with only himself. She was much better company.

When Sunday came, he woke and stared at the ceiling. "Today," he said. "Maybe you can kiss her today."

They hadn't had much time alone since Monday night, certainly nothing romantic enough that he could create a moment. He wasn't sure how to do it today, either, but she was planning to bring her brothers to the cabin for lunch. Sterling had bought frozen lasagna, and bags of salad, and two loaves of garlic bread.

He heard Norah come in upstairs as he finished

brushing his teeth, his choice of garlic bread suddenly weighing heavily on his mind. Maybe such a potent menu item would ruin the opportunity to kiss her.

Several more pairs of feet entered the house, further sinking Sterling's hopes. How could he kiss Norah with all her brothers around?

Voices came with the footsteps, and soon four more people joined him on the bottom level. "Morning." He smiled at the boys. "Let me see if I can remember…." He pointed to the oldest boy, almost as tall as Sterling. "Javier."

The teen beamed, and Sterling switched his attention to the next boy. He felt sure Norah had mentioned their names over the past month, but his memory failed him.

"That's Erik," Javier said, saving him. "And Alex."

Sterling snapped his fingers. "Erik, right. And Alex." He turned to Norah, who wore a short-sleeved dress with a belt around her waist. The skirt flared to her knees, one of those old-fashioned styles. Her long legs stretched down to a pair of heels, putting her closer to his height. He appreciated her beauty, loved the way she let her curls loose on Sundays when she normally tamed them into a tight poof on the back of her head for work.

"You ready for church?" he asked.

"Are you?" she teased.

"Oh, I am so ready." He employed every ounce of self-control he possessed to keep himself from reaching for her, tucking her against his side, kissing her.

Today, he promised himself. Somehow, he'd kiss her today.

"Thanks for letting us come for lunch." Norah's gratitude interrupted Sterling's thoughts, which lingered on something the pastor had said. He looked up from his phone, where he'd been reading the scripture the pastor had quoted. Norah stood at the window, her back to him, her arms crossed.

"Sure. Glad to have you." He didn't want to let her know how much he disliked being alone, how huge the house felt without someone there with him.

"Javier has the boys downstairs." She twisted toward him. "They've got a movie on. I told them it would be a while until lunch was ready."

"Couple of hours." He went down the two stairs to the living room, his leg aching only the slightest bit today, and collapsed into an armchair. "I'm so tired."

She joined him in the living room but sat in the other armchair, on the other side of the couch. "Nap time?"

"There are at least twenty beds here," he said. "We can definitely take a nap."

"Is your brother coming?" She picked her nails like she didn't care.

Sterling chuckled, wishing he'd chosen to sit on the couch so she could sit right next to him. "No, I've spoken with him several times this week. He's not coming today."

"One piece of good news." She glanced up and smiled.

Sterling stood and took a few steps toward her, an idea

forming in his head. "The boys will be busy downstairs for a while?"

Surprise and the tiniest bit of alarm entered her face. "Yeah, why?"

He extended his hand for her to take. "I want to show you something."

She rose and slipped her hand into his as the faintest hint of red kissed her cheeks. "Okay."

"It's upstairs." He started toward the staircase that led to the upper floor. "My mom has a library up here; you've seen it?"

"I dust it." The dryness in Norah's tone elicited another chuckle from Sterling.

"Of course you do. My mother is a freak about dust." Sterling had spent many Saturday mornings trying to appease his mother, claiming to have dusted picture frames and tables that she believed to still be covered in the wretched substance. He'd have to dust two or three times before she was satisfied.

"Have you ever looked at the books?"

"What kind of cleaning lady do you think I am?" They reached the top of the stairs, and Sterling steered her past the bunk bed room where she'd housed her girls, past one full bathroom and around to the end of the house.

"My mom keeps her most sentimental things here." He entered the library, really a bookcase-paneled room the size of a small kitchen. A tiny round table sat in the middle, flanked by two chairs. There was barely enough room to maneuver around the furniture to look at the books.

"She made all of us boys books for when we get married." Sterling released Norah's hand as he searched the shelves. "But then she couldn't give them away. Mine's obviously still here, but so are all my other brothers."

He located the volume and plucked it from the collection. Sitting in one of the chairs, he sighed. "You wanna see it?"

Her eyes shone with amusement, with anticipation. "Of course I want to see it."

Sterling smiled as he opened the book. "This is what my mother loved to do." He traced the first picture in the book —him as a newborn, only minutes after his birth.

"You had so much hair." Norah leaned over the book, wonder in her voice and her expression. Sterling showed her the pages, talked about his childhood, wanted to share that part of himself with her.

When they reached the end of the book, that sense of contentment filled him again. He wanted every afternoon to be like this one. Every evening to be filled with dinner and conversation with Norah.

As he sat in the silence of the library, he realized he was falling in love with Norah Watson. The idea both terrified and excited him. He'd never felt this secure with Amber. Never shared such personal things and had them accepted without question.

"I wish I had a book like that," Norah said, sadness in every syllable. She stood and replaced the tome on the shelf where Sterling had taken it.

He joined her, his heart beating at a screaming fast pace,

like a train off its tracks. "I'll make you a book," he whispered as he wrapped his arms around her. She turned into him, her hands sliding up his arms and into his hair.

Sterling didn't hesitate. Didn't question if this was the right moment or not. He leaned down and pressed his lips to hers, his blood on fire. She received his kiss eagerly, deepening it and pressing closer.

Sterling held on for dear life, grateful for the first time for the fall that had led him back to Gold Valley.

CHAPTER 10

Sterling lost himself to Norah's touch. Only she existed, even after they'd eaten, and played card games, and watched a movie. Even after she'd loaded up her brothers and left. Sterling lay in bed, his thoughts lost to the woman he'd first believed had broken into his house.

He closed his eyes and relived the pressure of her full lips against his. He wasn't sure how long they'd stood in the library, kissing, but it wasn't long enough. Especially since he didn't get to kiss her again before she left. Too many eyes.

She'd continue to drive him to Silver Creek each day, but he needed to figure out a way to spend more time with her in the evenings. Once a week wasn't going to cut it. Ideas percolated in his mind as he drifted to sleep, his dreams filled with coffee-colored skin, and strawberry-scented hair, and vanilla-mint lips.

The next morning, Sterling hurried to get ready so he

could make a phone call before Norah showed up. When Shelly answered at Silver Creek, he asked her for Norah's address. The secretary hesitated, and Sterling fumbled for a reason he needed it. One that wouldn't indicate he'd kissed a co-worker.

"I have something to send her mother," Sterling said. "And I want it to be a surprise." The statement wasn't entirely untrue. He did want to send dinner to Norah's house so she didn't have to cook. Maybe then she'd go out with him instead of rushing home....

"Well, isn't that sweet?" Shelly wore a smile in her voice, and a flood of guilt cascaded through Sterling as she rattled off the address. He wrote it down just as the garage door started to creak upward. He hastily ended the call and shoved the paper in his back pocket. He rarely saw Norah at work, so it shouldn't be too hard to arrange a dinner delivery without her knowing.

Convincing her to go out with him...that was another matter entirely.

He moved to the exit just as it opened. A grin burst onto his face, and he quickened his step, sweeping her into a hug. "Morning."

She giggled in response, pulled back a little, and stretched up to kiss him. This time was just as magical as the first, and he wanted to kiss her in every room in the cabin—and there were a lot of those.

Norah pulled away, her smile shy and her eyes downcast. "Ready?"

"I guess." Sterling wasn't keen on heading to the center,

where he couldn't touch Norah, couldn't kiss her, couldn't even look at her in a way someone might catalog as more than friendly. Now that he'd kissed her, he wasn't sure he could continue the charade.

But he zipped his lips and followed her to the car. With April almost upon them, some of the snow had started to melt into dirty slush, reminding Sterling of how much he disliked spring in Montana. Denver was much better, with a shorter winter and a cleaner spring. For a few minutes, he lost himself in his memories of living in the big city, with sponsors sending him gear every other day, and nothing on his mind but when he could get out to the mountain and snowboard.

That life seemed like it had ended years ago, not months. The familiar resentment and bitterness didn't come right away, didn't flood his mouth with a sour taste, didn't poison his mind and threaten to drive him mad.

The absence of those feelings surprised him, and he held them close so he could examine them later, when he was alone. When he was with Norah, he didn't want to be circulating things inside his mind.

He squeezed her fingers and asked her about school. "Only a few weeks until finals, right?"

She cast him a quick smile. "Right."

"How long until you're done? What are you studying?"

"I can take more classes in the summer," she said. "Because the boys are home to help more. Javier's graduating this year, but he'll stick around until fall."

"So how long?" Sterling asked.

"Another year, probably. Maybe a few last classes next summer." She pulled into the parking lot, and Sterling lamented the end of their hand-holding. At least for now.

He followed her down the path that led to the offices, but she veered toward one of the girls' buildings while he continued inside. Dr. Richards had asked him to make weekly reports, because of his leg. It felt much better; Sterling barely needed the brace anymore, though he still wore it, especially when he'd be standing all day. But he hardly took any pain medication, and the mobility seemed to be expanding.

After explaining all this to Dr. Richards, he went in search of Will and his boys. He found them in the cafeteria, eating breakfast. The space had been almost gutted, and a woman with red hair was directing a painting crew.

Will met him at the end of the table. "It should be done in a couple of months."

Sterling watched as a ladder got set up and the woman climbed the steps. "Does she paint?"

Will chuckled. "Belle is a hands-on designer. She'll be up there all day." He watched her, and Sterling noticed a look of longing on his face. "She finished the girls' dorms in record time."

"She's pretty," he said.

Will kept his focus on the redhead. "Don't get any ideas. She's taken. Married to the foreman at Horseshoe Home Ranch."

"Isn't that where you'll be working?" Sterling asked.

Will sighed. "Yep. Start in a couple of weeks." He tore his

gaze from the woman rolling gray paint on the walls and turned back to the at-risk boys. Sterling moved down to the end of the table and asked one of the boys, Lincoln, about the basketball game he'd been excited to watch over the weekend.

As the teen started to talk, Sterling noticed two of the boys further down the table start to become agitated. He kept one ear on what Landon said, but both eyes on the other boys. One stood; the other exploded to his feet.

Will didn't move a muscle, even when the first boy—Jack—threw a punch toward the second—Cooper.

Sterling couldn't sit here and do nothing. A hush fell in the cafeteria as the boys' voices escalated. Sterling hurried toward them, his heart thumping a mile a minute.

"Boys," he said. "Step away from each other."

Jack glared at him. "You're not the boss of us."

"Step back," Sterling said in his best police voice. "Trust me, you don't want to do this." He glanced at Cooper, the darker-haired teen. He hadn't been hit due to some great evasive maneuvers. Thank goodness.

"You hit him, and it's over for you, Jack." Sterling crossed his arms. "So step back. Cooper, you too. Right now. Together."

The two boys stared at each other, and seemingly with the same mind, stepped away from each other.

"Cooper, you stay with Will. Jack, take a walk with me." Sterling turned and headed toward the exit, not bothering to look to make sure Jack was coming. He would.

Sure enough, he passed the slower gait of Sterling and

slammed his palm against the door as he left the cafeteria. Sterling didn't mind. Better to let the boy get out his frustration on inanimate objects.

Jack practically ran ahead of Sterling, who didn't mind as long as he could see the boy. After several minutes outside in the weak sunshine, Jack returned to Sterling.

"Want to tell me what happened?" Sterling made his voice quiet, unassuming, careful.

"No."

"Do it anyway."

Jack exhaled, and Sterling felt the anger in him. It wasn't that hard to see, to feel, to recognize. Sterling had experienced it himself, those first few weeks—maybe until he'd met Norah—after the fall.

"You wouldn't understand."

"Oh, yeah? What wouldn't I understand?"

"You're rich," he said. "You don't get what it's like to—" Jack's face twisted into a scowl. "Forget it."

But Sterling didn't want to forget it. "I'm not rich. My family is."

"You were a gold medalist," Jack argued. "You had tons of sponsors."

"*Had*," Sterling emphasized.

"Whatever."

Sterling couldn't make him understand, and the fact was, he did still have a lot of money in savings. Better not to mention that, though. "What happened with Cooper?"

"He said my parents don't care about me."

Sterling frowned. "Why would he say that?"

"Because they're not coming for this weekend's parent weekend."

Sterling hadn't even known this weekend was parent's weekend. "And his are?"

"Of course. Mister I-Have-Everything-I-Want. He's from back east. Totally loaded." Jack kicked at the snow. "This is his third treatment program, and they're not cheap."

Sterling let the silence try to soothe Jack while he aligned things in his head. "And your family can't afford to come?"

"No," Jack muttered.

"Where do they live?"

"Tennessee."

Sterling didn't say anything else. After several minutes, he asked Jack where they were supposed to go next, and when he said, "The barn," Sterling took him there. Will had the rest of the boys already at work, so Sterling took the opportunity to slip away.

He hurried to the front office, thanked Shelly real quick for Norah's address, and knocked on the financial director's door.

"Come in," Rose Lovell called. Sterling pushed open the door to find her sitting at her desk. "How can I help you?"

He sat in one of the chairs opposite her, giving some relief to his leg. He'd seen the woman out in the stables last Monday, with a young teenage daughter. They'd been saddling a horse. He wasn't sure what they'd been doing, and he pushed the memories away in favor of a more pressing issue.

"How much would it cost to fly a couple of people here from Tennessee?"

Her eyebrows lifted into her dark hair. "Tennessee?"

"Yeah," Sterling said. "I want to pay to fly Jack Payson's parents here for the weekend."

———

Norah hung up the call from Javier, her stomach sinking at the same time warmth sang through her body. Sterling had asked her to meet him in the barn instead of at the car, so she entered the structure, expecting to see him hard at work with one of the horses.

Instead, he leaned against a stall, feeding a black and white horse sugar cubes from his palm. He chuckled as the horse's lips fumbled across his skin.

"Don't give 'im too much," Owen called from a few stalls down.

"Sterling." She marched over to him. "You sent a *catered meal* to my house?" Horror washed through her. Had he gone there? What had he seen? Did he meet Mama? She could barely swallow, and her stomach swooped up in a riot.

"Shh," he said, barely looking at her. "Yes, I sent some food to your house." He gave her a quick glance and lowered his voice even further. "I thought then we could go to dinner together."

She leaned away from him, one hip cocked, her arms

folded—mostly as she tried to keep her insides from quaking. "You're joking."

The horse gobbled up the last sugar cube. "I'm not." He wiped his hands on his jeans. "We can go to Missoula. No one there will see us."

"I can't drive an hour and a half—one way—for dinner." Did he think she was made of steel? That she didn't need to sleep? That she had gas money for such luxuries?

"Starvation, then."

That was still a half hour away. But the thought of spending time with him, eating alone with him, kissing him…. Norah let the idea play around in her mind.

"I'll pay for gas," he said. "And dinner." He paused as Tom Lovell came into the barn with his wife, Rose, and their daughter Mari. Norah stepped away from him automatically, like she couldn't even be caught talking to him.

"Hey, Rose," she said as the family approached. "Mari, are you riding tonight?"

"Yeah," she said. "My mom's going to have a baby."

"Mari," Rose admonished as Norah's eyes flew to the financial director at Silver Creek. She latched her hand in Tom's and beamed at him. "I guess it's not a secret anymore."

"Well, you tell Mari something, and you can't expect it to stay under wraps." The cowboy chuckled, and Norah smiled with them.

"Congratulations." She'd never given any thought to having a family, but one look at Sterling standing down the fence line, and suddenly all she could think about was having a house full of his sons.

Her own face heated as Tom helped Mari saddle a horse named Liquid Nitrogen. "Don't hold so tight," he told her. "Just because you're mad about the baby—"

"Not mad," Mari said, but she held the reins with a death grip. "Ride."

"Go on, then." Tom gestured for her to take the horse out to the arena. "Don't run him too hard." He watched her go, then stepped back to Rose's side. "She'll come around."

"You better go out there with her," Rose said. "She might run away."

He pressed a kiss to her forehead. "Nah, she'll stay where she's supposed to. Don't let her upset you." He strolled in the same direction Mari had gone, and Norah took the opportunity to head out too.

"Nice to see you, Rose." She glanced at Sterling. "You ready to go home?"

"Oh, Sterling." Rose stepped in between them. "Doctor Richards approved your donation."

Norah's eyebrows practically flew off her face. "Donation?" escaped her lips.

Sterling ignored her and thanked Rose. "I'm definitely ready to go home," he said. "Mondays are so exhausting."

"I heard that," Owen said as he came forward.

"No, you didn't." Sterling threw him a grin and followed Norah out of the stable. He kept a respectable distance between them, and though Norah didn't see anyone, she felt the weight of a thousand eyes on her and Sterling.

Once in the safety of the car, she asked, "Donation?" again.

"One of my boys needs his parents here this weekend. I asked Rose about making a donation for their airplane tickets."

Jealousy jumped through her. She'd needed someone like Sterling as a teen.

You need him now, she thought, and her envy ebbed away. It had been eleven years since her own parents' weekend, and she couldn't carry that resentment along with everything else she currently shouldered.

"Are you mad?" he asked as he took her hand in his.

The tension left her body, seemingly flowing out of her through the hand that Sterling held. "No, not really."

"So we can go to dinner?"

"You can't do this every week," she said sternly as she turned west, toward the tiny town of Starvation on the edge of Yellowstone National Park.

"Of course I can." He laughed, the sound bouncing around her small sedan.

"No, you really can't. I'm not going to let you send food to my brothers so we can go out."

"Well, they can't eat mac and cheese all the time."

"Exactly. We can't go out all the time."

"Norah."

She was sunk when he said her name so passionately, but she desperately tried to keep her face serious.

"I just want to spend time with you." He lifted her wrist

to his lips, sending a zing of electricity through her veins. "Is that so wrong?"

"No," Norah said. "But yes. We're not supposed to be dating."

"We're not at work right now."

"I can't lose my job."

"I'll quit before that happens."

"But we need you at the center too."

"Can we just not worry about it?" Sterling sighed. "At least for tonight?"

"Fine," Norah said, but the worry needled her, a constant buzz in her mind that wouldn't go away. She absolutely couldn't lose her job, and she knew Dr. Richards was counting on Sterling to run the at-risk group in only a few weeks.

She managed to soothe the anxiety in her gut with a Philly cheesesteak and the biggest Diet Coke Montana had to offer. And kissing Sterling under the stars drove out everything but the man holding her in his arms.

———

A couple of weeks later, Norah finished her work for the day—tons of paperwork as she prepared to say good-bye to one of her favorite groups of girls—and didn't have to drive Sterling back to the cabin. His brother had come to get him at lunch to take him to a doctor's appointment in Missoula.

She decided to swing by the building where Team Silver Bow lived, each girl sharing a room with another on the third floor. As she climbed the steps Norah hoped Sterling's appointment went well. He'd be asking the doctor if he could drive, and since riding a horse had been going so well, Sterling was hopeful.

Norah should be grateful too. Driving up the mountain twice a day—and back—had added a lot of miles on her car and extra minutes to her busy schedule. But in truth, she didn't mind. She loved the time alone with Sterling, the conversation that didn't center around teen addictions, the way he pressed her against the door that led to the garage and kissed her, kissed her, kissed her.

Pushing him from her mind so she could focus on her girls, she knocked on the first door. Her group should be packing for their departure tomorrow afternoon, and Norah made it a habit to stop by and help each one the night before she left. Her counselor had done that for her, and the memory still reminded her that someone, at some time, had cared about her.

"Hey," she said when Natalie opened the door. "How's the packing going?"

"Great!" Natalie bounced back into the room, her perma-grin stuck in place. Norah borrowed from the girl's enthusiasm, because packing night was always hard on her. She managed a smile before reaching for a shirt in a pile of clothes. "Who's is this?"

"Mine," Felicia said, her voice thick. She sat on her bed, as still as though she'd been frozen.

"Tell me about home," Norah said as she folded.

Silent tears tracked down Felicia's cheeks, but after a few

minutes, she began to talk. Norah listened, wishing she could wrap every one of her girls in a tight embrace and send them back out in the world with the reassurance that everything would turn out okay. But she couldn't.

After all, everything still hadn't turned out okay for her.

———

Sterling called while Norah was still in class. She saw the flashing indicator, saw his handsome face light up the screen, but she pushed the phone further into her backpack and concentrated on the lecture. With finals next week, she couldn't afford to be distracted during the review.

By the time the teacher finished and Norah escaped the classroom, he'd called twice more. As she walked toward her car, she swiped to call him back, her pulse palpitating. Maybe something had gone wrong at the doctor's office. Maybe he couldn't drive. Couldn't ride.

The line rang in her ear—and his ringtone sounded nearby. Norah shrugged it off as a coincidence—until the phone stopped ringing and he said, "Hey," and the ringtone in the parking lot cut off at the same time.

"Are you here?"

"Standing next to your car."

She peered through the lot, finally making out his tall form next to her sedan a few rows over and way down the line.

"How long have you been here?" She picked up her pace,

wishing she had automatic locks so she could at least offer him a place out of the wind.

"Only a few minutes. I had Rex drop me off here. I tried to call."

"I couldn't answer. It was the last class before finals."

"It's fine," he said. "I was just about to text when you called." His voice sounded in stereo, first through the line then through the streetlights.

"I'm going to hang up now."

"Rude," he teased. He added a chuckle to the word as she ended the call and stuffed her phone in her backpack.

She forced herself to walk instead of run. "Hey." She arrived at the car a little breathless, and not only from the brisk walk.

He slid his hands around her waist and brought her close. She leaned into him as he leaned against the car. "How's your leg?"

"Everything's better when you're here." He leaned down and kissed her with the slow precision she'd come to expect from Sterling. The man knew how to accelerate and brake at the same time, how to put pressure on the edges and make a turn, how to draw her closer without scaring her.

"Probably shouldn't have done that in public," he whispered. A grin pulled at his lips. "Couldn't help myself."

Norah enjoyed the safety she felt within the circle of his arms, loved the warmth from his body seeping into hers, the scent of crisp, Montana air mixing with the leather of his jacket and the spiciness of his cologne.

"Have you eaten?"

She tucked herself against his chest. "It's nine o'clock." Besides, she didn't want him buying her dinner every night. It had become a habit—one he didn't seem to mind, but one that had started to grate against Norah's conscience.

"Ice cream then."

"It's ten below zero."

"Well, I guess we can just stand here and kiss some more." He traced his lips along her temple, letting them fall to her earlobe.

Norah giggled, though a distinct tremor told her to take private things behind closed doors. "We can't do that. Come on, I'll drive you home." She stepped away from him.

"Can we at least stop for a soda or something?"

She moved around the front of the car and unlocked her door so she could flip the locks. "You and your midnight sweets."

"I won't be sleeping for hours anyway." He slid into the car with her.

"Oh, yeah? Why not?"

"The doctor said I could drive." Sterling took her hand in his and squeezed.

"Sterling! That's awesome news."

"Yes and no."

"No?" Norah wished the car would heat up faster, and she pressed the accelerator hard once she'd backed out. "Why no?"

"I won't get to ride to work with you anymore." He cleared his throat. "I won't get to see you at all anymore."

Norah didn't like the dark tone of his voice, though the

lost time with him weighed heavily on her as well. "We'll still see each other."

"Oh, yeah? When?"

"Well, since you've refused to stop sending food to my house on Monday nights, we'll be able to go out then."

"In Starvation, or Kenedee Falls."

"It's better than nothing." Norah didn't know how to reassure him. True, driving to remote towns where no one would see them dining had drawbacks. But it had perks too, like holding hands without the fear of someone seeing, or kissing over a shared brownie, as they had a few days ago in a tiny restaurant in an even tinier town.

"Norah."

She waited for him to continue, but he didn't. She passed Silver Creek and headed up the mountain, her nerves writhing against her muscles.

"The doctor said I can probably try snowboarding again." He delivered his words in a cool, even tone.

Norah's anxiety skyrocketed. "Do you want to snowboard again?"

He shrugged, and Norah refocused her attention out the windshield. Of course Sterling wanted to snowboard again. He'd been a gold medalist. A champion. His fall had been an accident—an accident that happened at the worst time, at the beginning of a promising career.

If he had the chance to snowboard again, she knew he'd take it over babysitting teen boys who didn't know how to tame their tempers and had gotten into trouble with weapons. She wasn't sure what had become of his police job, but she knew it had been put on hold for snow-boarding.

With a sinking, hollow feeling driving through her core, Norah knew everything in Sterling's life got put on hold for snowboarding.

Including his job.

His religion.

His relationships.

When she pulled into the cabin's driveway, she didn't open the garage and follow him inside like she normally would have.

"You're not coming in?" He turned toward her, his face half-lit by the motion-sensor bulbs along the garage.

Norah didn't know what to say, didn't trust her voice not to crack and break even if she did. Didn't matter what she said.

Sterling would leave Gold Valley, the way all the men in Norah's life had.

CHAPTER 11

A tornado of emotions twisted inside Sterling. He'd disappeared inside his own mind on the way up the mountain, much the same way he had on the way home from Missoula. The news that he could drive, that he could ride horses, that he could get back on a snowboard should've elated him.

And it did.

Honestly, it did.

But things seemed infinitely more complicated now too. He felt at war with himself, one half of himself urging him to stay in Gold Valley and see if things could go all the way with Norah, to focus on helping the at-risk boys he'd be getting on Monday, continue repairing his cracked relationship with God.

All of those things had brought his life purpose over the past several weeks. Purpose when he'd had none. A reason to get up, get moving, get happy.

And he was.

Honest, he was.

Happier than he'd been in a long time.

But not complete, whispered through his mind again, just as it had on the long drive home from the doctor's office.

And now Norah wouldn't come in. He really didn't want to leave her when things between them weren't perfect.

"What's going on in your mind?" he finally asked.

She shook her head, a few errant curls bouncing as she steadfastly kept her chin turned away from him.

"Norah."

"Stop saying my name like that."

"Like what?"

She finally faced him, a fire in her eyes that felt hot and furious and hurt and fragile all at the same time. He'd seen this look before, not on her face, but his. And seeing it on Norah's made his heart turn inside out.

"Like you adore me," she said. "It's hard to figure out what's true and what's not when you talk like that."

"I do adore you."

She shook her head again. "So, I guess you'll be moving back to Denver, then."

"Not for at least twelve weeks," Sterling said, deciding on the spot. He still had his apartment in Denver. His gear stored there. His friends—though he wasn't sure if he cared to see any of them again.

"Probably longer," he said. "Can't really snowboard in Colorado in July." He tried to make his tone nonchalant, like he totally didn't care or even know if he'd return to snowboarding. But something about the sport called to him, the stories the media would run about his comeback, the allure of being someone again.

Norah's shoulders relaxed, and Sterling banished his traitorous thoughts. "Please come in," he said, not above begging. After all, it had worked before.

She reached up and pushed the button on the automatic opener, and the garage door slid up. Sterling's heart seemed so heavy in his chest as she parked and killed the engine.

He got out first and went around to be there when she finally emerged from the car. "Let's not worry about what will happen in three months," he said. "Or six. Or never. Okay?"

She let him take her hand and lead her into the cabin. He took her past the kitchen, down the spiral staircase—which he could maneuver all by himself now—and to the couch in front of the fireplace in the basement.

"Pick a movie," he said. "I'll make a fire and hot chocolate."

"It's too late for a movie." She stood and rubbed her arms as if cold, though she still wore her winter coat.

He hated that she wouldn't just sit down, wouldn't relax. He should've known she'd react this way.

You shouldn't have told her about the snowboarding, he chastised himself.

But he'd wanted to. Wanted to share everything about his life with her. Sterling recognized the importance of this —that he wanted to hash things over with Norah and no one else. Even when Rex had asked if he'd snowboard again, only annoyance had soared through Sterling.

He'd watched five older brothers fall in love, and he recognized the signs within himself. But he also knew he wasn't there yet. And he had no idea where Norah stood. Sure, she seemed to like kissing him, and she seemed genuinely upset about the prospect of him leaving Gold Valley in favor of snowboarding.

He abandoned his plans to make hot chocolate and build a fire and hopefully snuggle up to Norah. He moved to stand in front of her.

"Tell me what's wrong." He ran his hands up her arms and back down, linking his fingers in hers.

She took a breath, her boxy shoulders lifting and falling too fast. "I don't really know. I just feel…."

Sterling peered at her, dipping his head to see her eyes as she ducked her chin to her chest. "Feel what?" He squeezed her fingers, hoping to reassure her that he was there, present, listening. That he cared.

She raised her chin and met his eye. "I don't see the point of having a relationship if you're going to leave in twelve weeks. Or six months." She dropped his hands. "And I'm not going anywhere."

"Norah, I'm not either."

"But you could be."

He exhaled. "If we live on could be's, we wouldn't do anything." Sterling paced back into the kitchen, turned, and tried to see her side. "I can train here in Gold Valley. I don't have to go back to Denver."

"So you *do* want to snowboard again." She wasn't asking this time, and Sterling didn't shrug.

"Yes, Norah, I want to try snowboarding again. But," he rushed to add, "I don't have to leave Gold Valley to do it. There are plenty of mountains here."

She blinked at him, new hope entering her eyes. "What if you get hurt again?"

"Then I build myself another nest of blankets and hope another beautiful woman breaks into my house." He kicked a smile in her direction, desperate for her to smile and laugh —and then kiss him before she left.

"I did *not* break in." She cocked a hip and folded her arms. "I had a key."

"Come here." He gestured her toward him, beyond glad when she came. He embraced her, holding her close to his heart for several long moments. "So we're okay?"

She melted into him, snaking her arms around his back and holding onto him too. "I'm just a little scared, Sterling."

"Of what, love?" He stroked her hair, the need to protect her growing to intense proportions.

She straightened and fell back a couple of steps. "So many things. Too many to get into tonight."

"Of me?" He closed one step of distance between them. "Of us?"

"Yes." She didn't mask any of her feelings, and Sterling saw them all. "I've never wanted to have a boyfriend, get married." A tear fell and she hastily brushed it away.

"Well, we're definitely to boyfriend." Sterling kept his face as placid as possible. "Want to tell me why you've never wanted a boyfriend? I mean, I think I'm pretty awesome."

A half laugh came out with her exhalation. "You are." She looked away. "It's a long story."

"I've got time."

Norah met his gaze with naked fear in her eyes. "I've never told anyone this story."

"Well, if you're gonna be my girlfriend, maybe you'll have to trust me." He gestured toward the couch. "Do you want to be my girlfriend, Norah?"

"Yes." Her mouth didn't move, and Sterling could've imagined the word. But the way his fingertips tingled and his body warmed, he hadn't.

Sterling stepped to the couch and sat in his usual spot, his instincts telling him that if he pushed Norah, she'd run. He said, "Then come tell me a story," anyway.

———

Norah sat way down on the other end of the couch, in the same place she'd chosen when the furnace had gone out. Now, she felt just as cold, but this chill existed on the inside instead of only being skin-deep.

"My brothers are only half-brothers," she started, using the flowered rug as a focus point. She let her eyes trace the vines up to the next rose. "Javier has a different father than the other two boys. Erik and Alex…their dad stuck around the longest." She shivered, though the furnace functioned and it wasn't that cold in the cabin.

Just thinking about their dad conjured up her headaches —and the escape he'd given her. She hadn't thought about Sterling's medication in weeks—since the orange pill bottles had disappeared from the counter.

She pressed her lips closed. She wasn't going to tell him about her addiction or her time at Silver Creek. Not tonight. Maybe not ever.

Maybe you'll have to trust me. His words looped in her head, causing her neck to tire from trying to hold everything in place. If she really wanted a future with Sterling, she'd have to tell him about her past love affair with hydrocodone and her first twelve weeks at the center.

Sterling's gaze felt heavy and soft on the side of her face, but she again traced the lines of the rug instead of looking at him. "Mama had been married to my father, but he passed away when I was a baby. After that…." She blew out her breath. "It was boyfriend after boyfriend, most of them stealing from us, or refusing to work, or sticking around until things got too hard for them."

Her fingers knotted together. "But no one ever really cared if things were too hard for me." A surge of resentment coated her insides with sticky tar, it's ever-present sickness. "After Cody—that's Erik and Alex's dad—left, Mama disappeared. She was diagnosed with her lung disease, and she suffers from major depressive disorder."

Finally feeling free and fierce, Norah looked up to find Sterling still watching her. Compassion and love radiated from his eyes. Nothing more. A muscle worked in his jaw, but he didn't speak.

"I've been taking care of everyone and everything for eight years." The traitorous tears came again, and this time Norah didn't wipe them away. "I'm tired, Sterling. And I've never wanted a boyfriend or to get married, because I've never seen it work out very well for Mama—or for me. Or for my brothers."

He got up and invaded her space, snuggling in close and wrapping his strong arms around her. He pressed a kiss to her temple and held her while she wept, not voicing that it would be okay, or trying to reassure her that boyfriends and husbands could be good too.

Theoretically, Norah knew they could. She knew Tom and Rose were happy. She'd seen Dr. Richards with his wife and two grown sons. She'd celebrated with Shelly and her husband for their twentieth anniversary.

But that happiness existed outside of Norah's sphere, and she'd always believed it would.

"I'm sorry," Sterling finally whispered. "No one should have to do what you do." He stroked her hair and kept his steady pulse pressed against her cheek. After she felt spent, she wiped her eyes and took a deep breath.

Sterling allowed a knuckle of space between them. "How about if you let me show you what a boyfriend can be like?"

Her pulse spiked. "What do you mean?"

"I mean, not all boyfriends steal. Or lie. Or leave. I can be trustworthy until you trust me."

"I do trust you," she said, though he only knew the tip of the iceberg of her life.

Tucking a piece of hair behind her ear, he smiled. "I

know you do, Norah. But you don't trust the idea of me, of us being together. And that's okay," he rushed to add. "I understand it'll take time. And like I said earlier, I've got time." He searched her eyes, trying to see something, but she didn't know what. "I just don't want you to give up on us before we can even start, because of something that may or may not happen."

Sterling leaned close, closer, his lips touching her neck just below her ear. "Okay, Norah?"

She nodded, the emotion spiraling through her now that of gratitude for this gentle man and his strong will. She had no idea she could speak freely with someone without the fear of judgment or the sting of rebuke.

"Thank you, Sterling." She leaned her forehead against his.

"You can tell me anything," he said. "I—" He cleared his throat and pressed his lips to hers. She wasn't sure what he'd been about to say—and if she were him, she'd prompt him until he told her—but she felt something new in this kiss.

Something joyful and wonderful and worth having. As she kissed him back, she struggled to identify what it was.

When she realized what she felt was love, she pulled back, utterly surprised that she could feel such strong things for Sterling so soon.

"What?" he asked.

"Nothing." She wasn't about to tell him she'd felt the first inklings of love for him. Not after only six weeks together. Maybe not for a long time.

She sighed. "I should go. It's late, and—oh, wait. I don't have to drive up here to get you tomorrow."

He sat back on the couch, keeping one arm around her shoulders. "Actually, I don't exactly have a car…." He rubbed the back of his neck and chuckled. "So can I get one more ride? And will you take me car shopping tomorrow?"

"Car shopping?" she asked. "Do you know how long it takes to buy a car?"

"Couple of hours?"

"More like all day," she said. "I'll have to bring my brothers, take them to lunch or something. They can't sit around the house alone all day."

"Bring 'em," he said. "I'll pay for whatever they want to do."

She cringed inwardly as she stood. "I am not telling them that. Javier will want to try the new virtual reality theater."

"I want to do that, too." Sterling joined her as she headed for the staircase. "He can try it if he wants."

"It's expensive," Norah said over her shoulder. Sterling already gave her too much gas money. She wasn't letting him foot the bill for her brothers' entertainment. Certainly not anything beyond a pizza or a hamburger.

Sterling kissed her again near the exit, the way he'd greeted her and said good-bye to her everyday for the past couple of weeks. "Bye, Norah," he whispered. Again, that new edge of love rode in his voice. Had she imagined it?

"Bye." She spilled into the brightly lit garage and hurried to her car while Sterling pushed the button to open the door.

It only took thirty seconds of the twenty-minute drive for her to convince herself she'd been hallucinating. "He doesn't love you," she said out loud. Number one, it was too soon for that, and number two, he was *Sterling Maughan.*

And she was nobody Norah Watson.

"Even dating him is laughable," she said, though they were definitely dating according to her standards. His too, obviously.

And if Dr. Richards knew she'd been kissing him for weeks, he'd think they were dating too.

Slow it down, Norah, she told herself, and not just because she needed to brake to take a hairpin curve as she came off the mountain.

CHAPTER 12

Norah spent most of Saturday night and Sunday morning battling herself. Turned out that buying a car with cash didn't take all day. Sterling walked in, picked out the truck he wanted, drove it for a few minutes, and wrote a check.

Wrote a check for twenty thousand dollars.

Norah had stared, dumbfounded at the numbers, at the way he scribbled his name, at the salesman who came back only ten minutes later with the keys and paperwork.

They'd breezed in and out within an hour and then gone for pizza—and the virtual reality theater. Alex was too young to go inside, so Norah had waited the hour with him while Sterling, Javier, and Erik "shot up the space aliens," and "had the best time of their lives."

"Is Sterling coming to church with us?" Javier asked as he came down the hall, straightening his tie.

"Not sure," Norah said, trying and failing to stop

thinking about Sterling. "I didn't talk to him about it." She had been driving up to the cabin to get him for the past several weeks. But the man owned a truck now, and he could get himself wherever he wanted to go.

Javier frowned. "Can I call him to find out?"

"Javier," Norah warned.

"What?"

"Let's leave him alone for a day."

He looked like he wanted to argue, but he didn't. Just got out the oatmeal and made a pot that would feed everyone. Norah couldn't help the well of admiration that gathered in her stomach as she watched him.

He could make it. He could take care of himself, and he thought about other people too.

"Heard anything yet from Montana State?" Norah usually kept up on what Javier had heard—she checked his email and monitored the mail. But she hadn't been doing that lately.

"I got in." He beamed at her.

A grin exploded across her face. "Why didn't you tell me?"

"I just got the email a couple of days ago. I got the needs-based scholarship too."

"Javier." Norah pressed one hand to her heart and willed back the tears. "That's so great."

"Yeah, only two years to my welding certificate."

Norah schooled her emotions. "Then move to California or something. Get out of here."

Javier glanced over her shoulder, where Erik and Alex

walked down the hall. "Thanks, Norah," he mumbled before dishing up breakfast for his younger brothers.

She knew what he meant when he said thanks. She could've asked him to stay in Gold Valley, find a technical trade school here, get a job, help with the bills and raising Erik and Alex. And when he said thanks, he meant *Thanks for letting me have my own life.*

It was a gift Norah wanted to give him, a gift no one had given her. But watching him interact with the younger boys, and with the memory of Sterling's words in her mind, Norah thought she might actually have a shot at living her own life one day. And she'd never felt like that before.

———

Sterling's skin itched, like he'd fallen into an anthill and couldn't get out. He sat in his new truck, the engine idling to keep the heater blowing, and stared at the front doors of the church. He'd arrived early, because if he hadn't left when he had, he knew he wouldn't go to church.

And he wanted to go to church.

Sure, he may have been coming just to see and spend time with Norah before, but now something deeper called to him, tugged on his desire to sleep in and shuffle around the house in gym shorts.

Getting himself to go in alone was proving much harder than he'd anticipated. He knew if he went inside, he'd be fully committed again. Sterling had always had a keen sense of right and wrong, and even after he'd let his religious side wither, he'd still known if what he said and did was good or not.

But if he recommitted, he'd have to live it. Not just *know* about right. But do right. Say right. Be right—as best as he knew how—everyday, all the time.

Families started arriving, and people moved through the bright sun and into the building. Sterling watched them without seeing, his mind still in turmoil with his spirit. When he caught sight of a tall boy walking next to a curly-haired woman, he straightened.

Javier and Norah led Erik and Alex down the sidewalk and into the church. Still, Sterling wrestled with himself. He didn't want to go to church because of someone else. He wanted to go because he wanted to be there.

Will I ever want *to be here?* he wondered.

Just go in and find out, came the answer.

Without hesitation, he yanked the keys from the ignition and jumped from the truck. He strode as best as he could, his head held high. In the chapel, he located Norah about halfway back, positioned between Javier on her left and the littler boys on her right.

He went to their row and leaned down. "You guys have room for one more?"

Javier's face lit up like a jack-o-lantern. "Sterling. Sure, man." He nudged Norah, who whispered for the other boys to move down.

Disappointment cut through Sterling that he couldn't sit next to Norah and hold her hand or smell her perfume. But that feeling evaporated under the narrowed gaze of Dr. Richards, who sat a couple of rows up and across the aisle.

Sterling lifted his hand in a friendly wave and focused his attention toward the pulpit. His heart thundered like a murderous Montana storm, but sitting with a family—not just Norah—couldn't be considered inappropriate. Could it?

He simply didn't want to sit alone, and he didn't know anyone else in town. No big deal.

The pastor got up and welcomed everyone to the Sabbath services. Sterling pretended to listen, but the words sounded muted behind the film of peace infusing his heart. He took a deep breath, and the weight he'd been carrying for the past several months lifted.

Gone. Just gone.

Like the Lord had taken it from him.

The strength Sterling needed, the strength he thought he lacked, was suddenly present. He closed his eyes as sudden emotion overwhelmed him.

Thank you, he thought. *Thank you for not giving up on me.*

After church, he leaned forward. "Norah, you guys want to come for lunch?"

"We can't—"

"Yes," Javier said at the same time Erik asked, "Can we, Norah?"

A pinch of guilt tripped through Sterling. He should've asked her privately instead of putting her on the spot. He flashed her an apologetic grin while at the same time his eyebrows rose. He really wanted her to come, and he knew she could. What excuse would she use and how could he circumvent it?

"Javier," she said through clenched teeth. "Remember what I said this morning?"

"What did you say this morning?" Sterling asked, finding Norah doubly desirable when she got fired up.

"Nothing."

"She said we needed to leave you alone for a day."

Sterling chuckled though he wanted to frown and ask Norah why *she* wanted a day off. "Norah should know by now that I don't like to be alone."

"Can we go, Norah?" Javier asked.

"Hey, you're eighteen, right?" Sterling thumped Javier on the knee. "Why don't you come? I'll grill us something."

Javier stared at him with wide eyes. "I'm not eighteen until the end of April."

"Close enough, man." Sterling refused to glance at Norah. He could practically smell the fury coming from her. "You're a senior, right? You won't have to check with Norah when you go to college."

Javier swung his attention from Sterling to Norah and back. "You got burgers?"

Sterling grinned, the scent of victory a lot sweeter than Norah's frustration. "Sure thing."

"He does not," Norah said. "Unless he went to the grocery store late last night."

Sterling lifted his eyes to hers, a teasing sparkle in his grin. "I happen to know where the store is, I'll have you know." He switched his flirtatious smile to a pleading look. "Come on, Norah. What was on your meal plan?"

He wished he could tell her he didn't want her to go back to her house, where her mom could cause new hurts and reopen old wounds. That he wanted her with him so he could ensure she was treated right, to make her happy, to show her how he could take care of her. The craving to do so made his stomach tight, and he swallowed to contain his emotion.

The chapel had nearly emptied, and still Sterling sat on the end of the row. Erik and Alex waited on Norah, and Javier broke the silence with, "I'm going. I'll take the boys with me. You can have an afternoon off, Norah."

Sterling's pulse missed a beat as it fell to his feet. "That's a great idea," he forced himself to say. "Take a nap, relax." Her declaration of how tired she was hadn't escaped Sterling. He knew she didn't just need a nap; she needed a lifestyle change.

"Fine." She stood and practically shoved the younger boys down the row toward the aisle opposite of Sterling. "We'll come. I can take a nap in one of your fourteen bedrooms."

"That's a great idea too!" he called after her, though the cabin only housed eight bedrooms, thank you very much. He glanced at Javier. "Did I push her too hard?"

Javier shook his head. "Nah. She needs it. She never does what she wants to do—and it's obvious she wants to go up to your cabin." He stood too and waited for Sterling to step into the aisle. "She just doesn't want to admit it."

Sterling followed Javier out into the lobby, where Norah helped the two younger boys put on their coats. She wouldn't look at him, and he turned to Javier. "You drive?"

"Yeah."

"Take Norah's car and follow me, okay?"

"I don't think—"

Sterling stepped away. "Hey, Norah. Javier said he'd drive Erik and Alex so you can come with me."

She squinted at him like she didn't quite understand English. "Javier can't drive up the mountain."

Frustration pooled with admiration in Sterling's gut. He reached for his jacket, brushing a bit too close to Norah to do it. "He's almost eighteen, Norah. He can drive anywhere he wants."

"You're maddening."

"You like it." He tossed her a grin, hoping she'd take his flirtation in stride. He moved away and put on his jacket. "Okay, I'm ready. Who's ready?"

The boys all looked at Norah, and Sterling realized her exhaustion could be partially self-inflicted. She nodded, and Alex, the youngest, cheered. "I'm ready, Sterling." He stepped next to Sterling, his face as radiant as the sun.

Norah passed the keys to Javier and said something under her breath. Javier responded in an equally quiet tone and herded the boys toward the door. Sterling wanted to draw Norah into a tight hug and kiss her until she melted into him the way she had before.

"You ready?" he asked instead, stuffing his hands in his jacket pockets.

"You're *really* maddening." She glared at him as she stepped in her high heels toward the exit. "You think you can get whatever you want because you're handsome, and charming, and rich." She slammed her palm against the door to push it open.

Sterling followed her into the near-noon sunshine. "You think I'm handsome and charming?"

She rolled her eyes as she clicked down the steps. "You know you are."

Happiness soared through him at her words. Though she'd been kissing him for weeks, it was still nice to hear that she liked him. He held the door for her while she climbed into the truck and adjusted her skirt.

"Norah," he said, leaning into the truck, her face at the same level as his.

"You can't keep doing this." She kept her attention straight out the windshield.

"Doing what?"

"Having us over all the time. Paying for everything. You'll spoil them."

"Its just lunch." He stepped away from her, sure she'd just implied that he'd spoil her brothers—and then leave town. He closed the door as she started to say something else and limped around the front of the vehicle.

Be patient with her, he coached himself as he got in the driver's seat.

"Look, Norah." He buckled his seatbelt. "I'm sorry, okay? Maybe I shouldn't have pushed you to come to lunch. But I want to spend time with you. Is that so wrong?"

She folded her arms. "I guess not."

"I'm not going to leave town, Norah." He started the truck. "And it sort of hurts that you still think I am."

"I don't think—"

"Then what did you mean when you said I'm spoiling them? Why can't I spoil them?"

"Because it's not their life," she said. "And it's not fair to make them think it is. Or that it could be. We're not all Sterling Maughan."

Sterling clenched his teeth, searching for the right response. "Well, I *am* Sterling Maughan, and I—I really like spending time with you, and those boys are good kids. If I can give them an afternoon in the game room and a hamburger, I'm going to do it." His fingers flexed on the steering wheel. "And you shouldn't be so upset about it."

He couldn't believe he'd almost told her he loved her. Words like that shouldn't be tossed around, and he swallowed them down to the bottom of his stomach. He may feel flashes of love for Norah, but she wasn't ready to hear that. He wasn't ready to say it either.

His phone rang as he turned onto the mountain road, and he flicked it on without looking at it. Norah hadn't spoken on the drive across town, and the tension in the car wasn't the kind Sterling wanted. He'd envisioned her sliding across the seat and cuddling into him the way country girlfriends did, the idea of being a cowboy boyfriend oddly alluring to Sterling.

"Hey," he said into the phone.

"Sterling," a man said, the voice instantly recognizable. "It's Gordon."

His sports agent and snowboarding career manager. He cut a glance at Norah. "Hey, Gordon. Now's not a great time."

"Okay, just one minute then." His agent had a knack for saying what he wanted to say, regardless of extenuating circumstances. "I need you in Denver this week."

Every cell in Sterling's body wanted to hang up, and hang up now. Norah seemed perched on her seat, though she hadn't moved.

"I can't," Sterling said. "I have a job here."

Gordon scoffed. "The rep from Burton wants to renew your sponsorship. She's convinced you'll be back on the slopes next winter. I'm not gonna tell her yes or no either way. She needs your signature so you can get paid."

Sterling almost pumped his fist. It knocked against the steering wheel instead, and he quickly released his fingers and re-centered them so he didn't drive off the road. "That's great, Gordon. Can't you email me the docs? Or fax them over?"

"Libby wants to meet with you." He sighed. "I think she's going to try to get an answer from you one way or the other. You need to sign first."

Sterling thought as fast as possible. "Okay, how about you fax me the pages to sign, and I'll send them back tomorrow. Then I'll come in on Saturday to meet her. So the paperwork will already be done before she gets to talk to me."

Gordon chuckled. "I really need you to be my protégé." He'd offered to train Sterling in sports agenting before, but nothing about the job had appealed to Sterling.

"Not gonna happen." Sterling glanced at Norah. Especially now.

His agent exhaled, like he wasn't happy with Sterling's answer, or that he wouldn't come to Denver until Saturday. "I'll see if I can get Nordica to renew too," he said. "Several reps will be in town for the end of the season awards."

Jealousy jumped against the back of Sterling's throat. "Sounds great, Gordon. Keep me in the loop." He hung up, his hopes for the future higher than they'd been since he'd won gold.

"Who was that?" Norah asked, her carefully masked interest in his conversation almost cute.

Sterling grinned. "My agent." He wanted to share everything with Norah, without worrying her.

"You're happy about whatever he said."

He tried to straighten his lips and couldn't. He trusted Norah with his news. So he told her.

CHAPTER 13

An invisible raincloud followed Norah around the cabin, though she pretended like she was having fun. Sterling did know how to make a mean hamburger, though the grill pan he put over two burners had surprised Norah.

Alex and Erik loved the pinball machine in the game room, and Javier had stolen Sterling's attention as they played game after game of pool. Norah escaped up to the third floor—to the bunk bed room—after catching Sterling's eye and pointing to the ceiling.

She lingered in the library, her fingertips brushing her lips lightly as if every part of her remembered the kiss that had happened here. The kiss that had changed her life.

Feeling tired, and overwhelmed, and somewhat grouchy, she entered her favorite room in the cabin and selected the bed farthest from the door and closest to the window. She sat on the homemade quilt and pulled her knees to her chest, her gaze out the window. The view boasted snow-heavy pines, a sky the color of blue raspberry popsicles, and a horizon for miles and miles.

The raincloud lifted, leaving a sense of peace Norah craved. She'd never been able to find it at her house on the other side of the tracks. The closest she came was at Silver Creek, but even then, the pressure of being there for the money didn't allow her to truly relax, to truly enjoy herself, think about her life.

Here, with silence as her only companion, Norah felt whole. She always had, which was why cleaning Six Sons Cabin had never felt like a chore. Every week, she'd sit on this bed and look at this view and dream of a life outside the confines of Gold Valley.

As they always did, her thoughts wandered to Mama. She hadn't called or texted. She wouldn't, because she never came out of her room on Sundays.

Though she'd come grudgingly, Norah recognized the happiness flowing through her. She dipped her head and offered a prayer of thanksgiving for the blessings she enjoyed—including the addition of Sterling to her life.

With positive emotions parading out the negative, she slipped under the quilt and closed her eyes. She never enjoyed a Sunday afternoon nap, and as she drifted into unconsciousness, she realized the gift Sterling had given her.

———

Monday morning dictated that Norah arrive early to be ready to welcome her new girls to the center. Counselors lined the sidewalk along the circle drive, and she caught Sterling's eyes as he waited at the very end. The at-risk boys always arrived last. Dr. Richards and his key staff took the twelve-passenger vans to the airport on Sunday evening so they could be ready for the early-morning flights, leaving Lori—the most senior counselor on-staff—in charge.

She walked the line, handing a clipboard to each counselor. When Norah got hers, she glanced at the eight names that represented the girls she'd be meeting in half an hour. She didn't expect to recognize any of them, and she didn't. She never read the individual sheets until the end of the first week, wanting a chance to get to know the girls outside of what had brought them to the treatment center. Another tactic she'd learned from Kathy, the counselor who'd felt more like a mother to Norah.

The first van arrived, and their counselor stepped forward to help her girls with their luggage. As one vehicle pulled away, another turned in. Dr. Richards had perfected the system so that each group had their moment, a chance to get settled without having to be overwhelmed by the size of the grounds or the number of people on-site.

When it was Norah's turn, she turned on her smile and opened the van doors. The first girl she saw sported ginger hair and the most beautiful freckles Norah had ever seen. "Welcome to Silver Creek. Take your bag and line up along the curb." She reached for the bag nearest the door.

"Don't touch it," a girl in the back row growled. Half of

her head had been shaved, and she glared with all the fury of a caged wolf.

Norah pulled her hand back. "Larger suitcases will be delivered to your rooms this afternoon. I'm Norah Watson and I'm your scheduling counselor while you're here at Silver Creek. That means I'll take you to your activities, your appointments, your meals. I am not a doctor, but you can talk to me, and I'll listen."

The freckled girl gave her a timid grin, reached for her bag, and stepped out of the van. By the time the girl in the back got out, Norah knew her name. "Welcome to Silver Creek, Paige."

"Yeah, yeah. Save it, Norah."

But Norah wouldn't save it. Even if Paige didn't want to be here, Norah would make sure she had the best experience possible. After all, she hadn't wanted to enroll at Silver Creek, but it had changed her life.

She led the girls down the sidewalk, talking about the meal schedule and pointing out where the cafeteria bulged out the side of the front office building. The construction and remodeling wouldn't happen today as Dr. Richards had made sure everything was as peaceful and easy as it could be. Norah indicated the barns and spoke about the horses.

"Will we ride today?" one of her girls, Harriett, asked.

"Not today," Norah answered. "But our team is scheduled for tomorrow afternoon."

She spent the morning outlining the center's rules and policies, which the girls had already received through the mail but if they were anything like her, they hadn't read them. She monitored their lunch and returned them to their shared dorm rooms to unpack that afternoon. Even though she didn't do much physically, by the time she got the girls to dinner, where the night staff would then combine all the groups for an evening activity before lights out at nine p.m., Norah felt ready to drop.

She hadn't seen Sterling once, not that she expected to. The at-risk boys had a separate residence tucked behind the stables, as they worked with the horses, and they didn't mix with the rest of the residents until the second week.

Feeling hungry and a bit lost, Norah sat in her car. She and Sterling had gone out every Monday night for weeks. But they hadn't talked about tonight, nor did she know when he'd finish with his boys. She'd never really paid much attention to what the male counselors did.

Her phone buzzed and Javier's message made her spirits lift. *I texted Sterling to tell him thanks for the sandwiches. Have fun tonight.*

They'd never talked about where Norah went on Monday nights, but Javier had obviously put two and two together. Norah hoped he was the only one, and that he wouldn't say anything to anyone else. Certainly not anyone that could mention it to Dr. Richards.

Deciding to wait until Sterling got in touch with her, Norah reclined her seat and closed her eyes. She wasn't sure how long she dozed, but the ringing of her cell woke her. The tone cut off, spiking her heartbeat. A moment later, as she fumbled for the phone in her purse, the sound started again.

"Hey," she said, wiping her eyes. "Where are you?"

"Just finishing up. I sent sandwiches to the boys, and I thought we'd eat in tonight."

"Oh, yeah? Grilling again?"

He laughed, the sound absolutely infectious and causing a smile to form on Norah's face. "No," he said. "I hope you like turkey on sourdough."

"I actually do."

"So, you want to follow me up?"

"Sure, you already on your way?" The sun didn't set quite as early as it used to, and Norah found herself looking forward to the warmer weather.

She started the car as he said, "Just pulling out."

"See you in a few." A quick prick of guilt hit Norah behind the eyes as she checked the parking lot for Dr. Richards' car before she turned right toward the exclusive cabin community instead of turning left and heading to her house.

She needed to deal with the co-worker issue, and soon. She added it to the list of things she needed to address sooner rather than later, including talking to Sterling about his return to Denver and her own struggle with a dangerous substance.

He'd been tender and kind since her confession about her mother and her string of boyfriends. His behavior hadn't exactly changed, but it was a load she didn't have to carry alone anymore, and that alone meant the world to her.

At the cabin, she found him on the main floor, sitting at the kitchen counter, a spread of sandwiches, fruit, and potato chips in front of him. "I got those sour cream and cheddar ones you like." He picked up the bag an inch or two and let it fall back to the counter.

Her mouth watered at the same time her stomach tightened. She stepped next to him, trying to bury her nerves, and kissed him. The warmth of his hand along her waist and the strength and softness of his mouth knocked her down another rung. She pulled back and selected the middle piece of the sandwich and put it on a paper plate.

She hadn't pushed him about Denver yesterday, though he'd seemed to talk and talk until he ran out of words to say. But she wanted more. "So you're flying out Friday night?"

"Late," he confirmed. "I didn't want to leave work early the first week." He took a bite of his sandwich, seemingly at ease as he chewed and swallowed. "I won't be back until Sunday evening. Think you'll survive church without me?"

"Oh, please." She opened her favorite chips. "It's Javier that'll need shock treatment."

"He's a great guy," Sterling said.

"He thinks the world of you." Norah settled next to him and started eating, starting to feel more at ease though that irrational fear that he'd jet off to Denver and stay remained.

They ate, and he talked about his first day alone with his boys, and she worked up the courage to voice her fears. "What time will you be back on Sunday?"

Sterling surely heard the undercurrent of emotion in her voice. She couldn't have concealed it if she'd tried. "Look, I'll be honest. I'm worried you'll get back to Denver, and like it there, and not want to come back here."

And that wasn't even the tip of what she worried about. His fancy apartment, the call of other pro snowboarders in town, meeting with his agent. Norah didn't know what else could pull on him, get him to stay.

"Norah." Her name in his voice said so much, but it didn't quite reassure her the way she wanted it to. "I'm coming back. I have a job here. I wouldn't let those boys down."

She nodded. "I know. You're right." She reached for his hand, laced her fingers between his, and gave him a closed-mouth smile. Though she was glad he wouldn't let the at-risk boys down, she wanted him to say he'd come back for *her*.

"My flight gets in at six-forty-two," he said. "Flight 6445." He leaned over and kissed her, driving her concerns to the back of her mind. "I'll call you when I'm boarding."

"Sure, okay." Norah put on her happy face, mostly reassured. She'd been praying to learn to trust Sterling, and she offered the same lines again. She didn't want to lose him because she couldn't figure out how to trust him—and she knew he wouldn't give her forever to figure things out.

But hopefully a little longer.

———

Friday, Sterling's leg ached with a ferocity he hadn't endured for weeks. He popped three ibuprofen after he parked at Silver Creek, his gaze fixed on the cabin where his boys lived. Harvey, a tall, skinny kid of fifteen, stood on the porch, sweeping under the watchful eye of the night counselor, Wade.

He looked ready to drop, so Sterling got out, locked up his truck, and strode toward the cabin. At least his new cowboy boots didn't pinch anymore. Owen had spoken true—it had only taken a few days to break them in.

A few days on your feet twelve hours a day, Sterling thought as he spied Owen loitering in the chair next to the door of the barn, his guitar resting across his lap, the last chords he'd played still reverberating in the chilled morning air. Sterling raised his hand in greeting, but continued toward the cabin.

"Mornin', Wade." Sterling tucked his cowboy hat on his head, feeling very much like the wrangler he was pretending to be. Eventually, he thought maybe he'd really be a horseman, instead of just wearing the clothes and faking the accent.

"Sterling." Wade wiped a hand over his face, a clear sign of his exhaustion.

"Harvey," Sterling said, turning to the boy sweeping. "You pull dawn duty?"

The dark-haired boy met his eye, and Sterling couldn't believe he'd used a pair of scissors against a classmate. "Volunteered, Mister Maughan. Owen said if I swept every morning, I could saddle all the horses."

Sterling leaned against the railing of the cabin and looked toward the barn again. Owen had disappeared. "And that's something you want to do?"

Harvey shrugged. "I like being with the horses."

"Me too," Sterling murmured, recognizing the feeling for the first time. "How long 'till you're down there?"

Harvey bent and swept up his pile. "Done now, sir."

"I'll stay here and get the other boys up," Wade offered. "Not supposed to be off for another half hour anyway."

Sterling nodded at him, knowing that part of Wade's shift was to get the eight boys up and ready for the day before Sterling arrived.

He wandered over to the barn with Harvey, the sense of silence and stillness surrounding them speaking to Sterling's soul. In Denver, he'd surrounded himself with people, and noise, and lights. Here, none of that existed. No one cared what he'd eaten for breakfast, or which horse he preferred.

"Mornin'." Owen stepped out of the tack room, his white cowboy hat perched low over his eyes. "You ready, Harvey?"

"Yes, sir." The boy stood a little straighter.

"All right, then." The cowboy thumbed behind him. "Everything we need's in here. You have to be calm around the horses. No temper when things don't go right. No sudden movements. Think you can do that?"

"Yes, sir."

Owen's eyes ran from Harvey's face to his feet and back as if appraising him, judging him. "All right, then. Let's get started. Sterling, ole Red is down at the end. She's already waitin' for ya."

Sterling waited until Harvey stepped into the tack room with Owen, then he continued down the aisle to the tall, burnished red horse waiting for him in the last stall.

"Hey, Red." He stroked both hands down the side of her face, comforted simply by touching the horse. "Did you have a good night?" He brushed back her hair. "Who's gonna ride you today, huh? One of the girls, I bet."

The horse didn't answer, of course. Horses never did. But Sterling felt someone speaking to him, infusing him with peace. He bowed his head and prayed for strength to endure this weekend, his agent, his sponsors, and being so close to snowboarding without losing what he'd found these past several weeks.

Without losing himself—again.

The plane touched down just before midnight, the flight having been delayed for an hour on the runway in Montana due to high winds. Sterling's stomach felt so tight, he hadn't been able to even enjoy his peanuts. In fact, the salty snack now swirled in his gut like poison.

Gordon waited near the baggage claim, but Sterling carried everything he'd brought. "You made it." Gordon grinned like Sterling had just won another gold medal. "And you're barely limping. Though, I can tell you are. We'll need to make sure you're in the room before the reps arrive. Then it's just legal talk and a few questions, and you can stay seated until they go."

Sterling managed to grunt a passable response, suddenly aware of every traveler in the airport. At least none of them were reporters that he could see. But he didn't like the unsettled feeling that now people would be judging how he walked. He longed to return to Gold Valley and forget about snowboarding completely.

At the same time, his signature on the paperwork Gordon had faxed earlier that week meant he could buy a house in Montana—for cash. And a certain level of expectation came with that much money.

He took a deep breath as a cab pulled up to the curb and Gordon ushered him into it. Sterling could shoulder this. He had before.

With a text on its way to Norah—who wouldn't get it until morning—Sterling admired the bright lights of the city he used to love. He still loved Denver. Maybe not everything that had happened here, but the metropolis possessed a pulse he could feel even this late at night.

Once at his downtown apartment, sealed behind a locked door, Sterling finally relaxed. His meeting with the brand reps wasn't until late morning, and he walked his apartment, remembering his life in Denver.

Not all of it was bad.

But none of it included Norah, and Sterling wondered if his connection to her could overcome the call of returning to snowboarding, to Denver.

He settled at the kitchen counter and pulled out his laptop. He confirmed with his realtor that he wanted to meet at nine a.m. the next morning, but the thought of listing this apartment—of selling it and never being able to come home to it again—introduced a nest of snakes to his already swirling gut.

He sighed and stood up, leaving his laptop on the counter as he went into his bedroom. "It's Norah or Denver," he muttered as he pulled off his shirt and pants and slipped into his gym shorts. "Can't have both, Sterling." He fell into bed, still oscillating between which one called to him the loudest.

———

The next morning, a knock had him hurrying from his bedroom. He slowed and evened his gait before opening the door. He didn't even want his realtor to see him limping. No one could know, because then everyone would know.

He pulled open the door, ready to gesture the woman into his apartment. But the woman standing in the hall wasn't Irene Goodsell, the realtor that had sold him this downtown gem.

Instead, a blonde twenty-something stood there, wearing skin-tight jeans and a fluffy white vest over a long-sleeved red T-shirt.

"Amber." The word scraped against Sterling's throat, searing his tongue. He didn't recognize the sound of his own voice.

"Gordon said you'd be back last night." She pouted at him. "You didn't call."

Confusion and frustration puckered his eyebrows. "Why would I call?"

"I left you about a dozen messages." She folded her arms. "Can I come in?"

"No—"

She stepped past him despite his protest and headed into the living room. "This place hasn't changed a bit."

Sterling left the front door open, not wanting to be trapped in a closed space with this woman. "Neither have you. You need to go." He'd never felt something so strongly before.

"I have changed." She dropped onto the couch. "Which you would know if you'd answered my calls."

He leaned against the wall near the door, unwilling to get any closer. "I blocked your number, Amber. I heard everything I needed to hear." And so much more. Leaning against the doorway, watching her with lasers shooting through his eyes, Sterling didn't want to waste any more time on Amber. He hadn't six months ago, and he certainly didn't now.

"You should go," he said again as she opened her mouth to say something. "I don't have anything to say to you." Behind him, the elevator chimed, and he prayed with every-thing in him that it would be Irene.

"Knock, knock," the realtor said, and relief sang through Sterling.

"Come in," he said to her. "Amber was just leaving."

Irene spotted Amber as she stood from the couch, and surprise lifted the real estate agent's brows. "Am I inter-rupting?"

"More like saving me," Sterling hissed as Amber came closer. "Good-bye, Amber." He spoke with such finality, she couldn't misunderstand him. And Irene was here to corroborate.

The blonde he'd once found so alluring, so sexy, so sincere, flounced to the elevator and practically punched the call button. The doors slid open, she stepped onto the car, turned and glared at him, before the elevator closed and removed her from his life. Hopefully for good.

Sterling exhaled. "Hello, Irene."

"So, you want to put this apartment on the market?" Irene breezed past the kitchen and into the living area. "It's an amazing place," she continued. "We shouldn't have a problem getting a good price for it."

Sterling felt like a door in his life was closing and wouldn't be opened ever again. At the same time, God had opened other doors for him, and he needed to choose the right one.

"Make it happen," he told Irene. "And I need you to connect me with someone good in Gold Valley. I'm going to need a place there."

She nodded, though the set of her mouth and the angle of her eyebrows suggested she had many questions for him.

He had a lot too, but moving to Montana wasn't one of them. With that burden lifted, he made it through the walk-through with Irene, the intent to list paperwork, and over to his agent's office on time to meet the brand reps.

CHAPTER 14

$\mathcal{N}$orah dusted and swept and mopped and cleaned toilets for Gold Valley's wealthy. The winter was definitely not the busiest time, but now that April flirted with May, several families had started to come back up to the mountains. And summer would be insane, when they'd come back to escape the oppressive heat of their regular homes.

She thought of Sterling constantly, disdainful that even her loudest music couldn't drive him away while she worked. She wondered if the meeting with his real estate agent had gone well, if his sponsors had squeezed the information they wanted from him, if his late-night text was really true.

Missing you so much. See you soon.

He'd sent the message just after midnight, and she hadn't gotten it until that morning, when she'd woken. The fact that she wouldn't be able to see him that evening ate a hole through her, and she hadn't known how to answer his message. So she hadn't.

She stewed over what he might think of her silence. She considered bringing him home to meet her mama, of seeing where she came from. The idea didn't strike as much fear in her as it once had, but then she arrived at Six Sons to do her weekly cleaning. Thoughts of the differences between his house and hers had her tongue back in knots.

You can't tell him, she lectured herself as she straightened the kitchen upstairs. She noticed a flashing light on the phone system, and she pressed the button without thinking. Of course it would be Nancy, who called the cabin when she had something to say to Norah.

"Norah, hello." The woman's voice oozed with warmth and money. "I'm sending a client up to the cabin next weekend, so please make sure the master is stocked by Friday night. I'll transfer funds to your account for toiletries and groceries and I'll email you a list. Please confirm when you get these items." A pause followed Nancy's carefully recited message. "I'll let my son know he needs to find somewhere else to be next weekend. This is an important client. Well, okay, thank you, Norah."

Norah's first thought was where Nancy thought Sterling would stay. Maybe a hotel. They certainly were the family that could pay for endless nights in a hotel. Then she wondered how long it would take to erase his presence from the cabin by Friday night. True, the top two floors barely showed someone lived there, but the basement spoke a different story.

She finished her work and flipped on the TV in the master bedroom, as she'd done many times before. She made a list of what the bedroom needed to be ready for a guest as the television provided background noise.

"Sterling Maughan," caught her ears. She turned from the bathroom, where she was folding towels and checking the levels of shampoo.

The television showed a picture of Sterling, pre-fall. Suntanned and stunning, his smiling face took up the whole screen.

"The snowboarder who suffered a serious fall only six months ago has emerged from hiding. He was spotted in downtown Denver today, reportedly on a way to a meeting with several of his sponsors. And Dave, that has everyone on the slopes talking."

"It sure does, Marty." The camera switched to the male sportscaster, who continued to speculate on when Sterling would announce either his retirement or his return to the sport he so clearly had loved.

Norah's legs gave out and she sat on the bed. Sterling did love snowboarding. He'd been really, really good at it. Her mind tumbled back to the first time they'd met: the unwashed quality of his hair, how he hadn't shaved in days, the nest of blankets on the couch downstairs.

"He's a snowboarder," she whispered to herself. A sense of forgiveness washed over her, though she couldn't quite make sense of the emotion. But she suddenly knew she couldn't change him—didn't *want* to change him.

But she also knew with absolute certainty that she'd

fallen in love with a snowboarder—not the handsome cowboy-counselor he'd started to become. But a snowboarder. Because Sterling Maughan would always and forever be a snowboarder first.

———

Norah stopped by the barn on Wednesday after dropping her girls off at dinner. Sterling rode late on Wednesdays, it being his night for a private riding lesson with Owen.

He was already atop a beautiful reddish-brown horse Norah had seen on occasion. Red, she thought the horse was named, and appropriately so. With a friendly wave, she put one foot on the bottom rung of the fence and watched as he trotted the horse in a figure-eight pattern.

Owen spoke in soothing tones, the same as always. Norah had seen Sterling in his jeans, boots, and cowboy hat on several other instances. But something about him now, sitting in the saddle and maneuvering the horse around the arena with barely a twitch of his fingers ignited something inside her.

He'd become a cowboy. A smile twitched against her lips. She'd always fancied herself with a cowboy, if she was going to be with someone at all. And since Sterling had called her as he boarded his flight, and as she'd kissed him hello after two days apart, Norah knew now she did want to share her life with someone.

Not just someone. Sterling Maughan.

She hadn't told him any of that, though. She hadn't

invited him to meet her mother, or to see her house, nor had she confessed about her teen drug addiction.

It could all wait, she'd reasoned. Sterling, after all, wasn't going anywhere.

"Norah?" Dr. Richards' voice startled her away from the fence. She quickly attempted to wipe away the admiration surely showing on her face.

"Doctor Richards," she said.

"I don't normally see you hanging around after work," he said, his gaze moving from her to where Sterling rode in the arena. A frown pulled at the corners of his mouth.

"I was just heading out," Norah said, thinking quickly. She didn't want to lie. "I saw Owen in here, and I thought I'd see why. I didn't know he gave private lessons."

Fine, that was pretty much a lie. Norah knew Owen helped the new counselors become horse-worthy, especially the at-risk counselor.

"He's coming along, isn't he?" Norah turned back to watch Sterling for another moment. "How's he doing with the boys?"

"Really well, actually." Dr. Richards joined her at the fence. "I was just going to check in with him after his lesson. Do you think he's enjoying the work?"

"I don't know," Norah said, and at least that was the truth. Sterling had spoken of his boys a little bit at the beginning of last week, but not much since then. It seemed as both of them experienced enough of the stress and sadness surrounding their patients at work that neither of them wanted to hash it over afterward.

"Well, I should go," Norah said with a glance to Dr. Richards. "Good-night, Doctor Richards."

"'Night, Norah." He didn't look away from Sterling this time, and Norah escaped from the barn without having to answer another question. Feeling as if she'd dodged a speeding bullet, Norah hurried to her car, knowing with every step that she needed to confess her relationship to Dr. Richards.

Soon.

Sterling, however, didn't agree when she brought it up to him on Friday after work.

"It's a dumb policy," he said as he threw things into an overnight bag. "Let's just wait a little longer."

"Wait for what?" Norah stacked new boxes of soap and bottles of shampoo and washcloths she'd carefully folded into triangles. He'd accompanied her to the grocery store, and together, they'd unloaded the groceries and stocked the refrigerator upstairs for his mother's guest.

And he was leaving for Denver that night. Again. His apartment had sold after only twelve hours on the market, and his realtor needed him to sign papers. He wanted to hire a moving company, and he needed to be out of the apartment by the end of June.

"You're still good to help me look at a place on Monday night, right?" He glanced up from his phone, which rang and chimed a lot more than it used to.

"Yes." She watched him thumb out a response and hit send. "Okay, I told Miles to expect us."

"What are you looking at?" She made sure not to say the

word *we*. She wasn't looking for a place to live *with* him. She wasn't even sure why he wanted her to come.

"A couple of houses on the north end of town."

"Up near the canyon?"

"Yeah, you know the area?"

"I've lived here my whole life," she said, trying not to let any sarcasm enter her voice. She didn't entirely succeed. "There're new developments going in."

"Yeah, a couple of those. I guess there are a couple of models to choose from."

"Those won't be ready for months." She finished her work and gripped the handles of the basket she needed to lug up two flights of stairs so she could finish getting the house ready.

"Fall, at least. Mom said I could stay here until then." He zipped his bag. "They won't be back in the country until the beginning of September anyway. I guess a couple of my brothers are using the house this summer, but I can find somewhere to crash while they're here."

He hooked her eyes with his. "Hey, on Monday after we look at the houses, maybe you'd like to show me *your* house." He hooked his thumbs through her belt loops and pulled her closer. He smiled down on her, but Norah's heart felt like a herd of wild horses thundering through the woods.

"My house?"

"Mm." He leaned down and kissed her, slow and careful, amping into something more passionate and dangerous with every passing second. Normally, Norah would pull back when she felt this level of desire stemming from him, but now she matched the intensity and movement of his lips with her own. Desperation coursed through her, though the moment called for her to focus on Sterling.

As his heated hands met the bare skin of her lower back, Norah managed to break the kiss. He nuzzled her neck, never pushing too far, but his desire for her obvious in his touch, in the heaviness of his breath, in the pressure against her back.

"So?" he asked. "What do you think? Think you're ready to take me home to meet your mom?"

She gazed into his dark eyes, so open and so trusting. She marveled at the strength in him, the beauty, the kindness.

"I love you," she whispered, unable to tell him he could come to her wrong-side-of-the-tracks home and meet her clinically depressed mother.

A half-smile quirked his mouth. "I'm sorry. I didn't quite catch that."

But he had heard her, and she matched her smile to his. "Sterling—"

"I love you too, Norah." He rendered her silent with those words and when they kissed, she allowed herself to focus entirely on the shape, the feel, the heat of him next to her.

———

Sterling existed inside a warm bubble he imagined to be sunny and yellow and beautiful. Because Norah had said she loved him. And he'd been able to say it back—and mean it.

He floated through security in Denver, his driver waiting at the top of the stairs as he came gliding up. He spent the night in his apartment, and passed the hours the next day boxing up everything he wanted the movers to bring to Montana.

The time he devoted to his phone seemed endless. First to set up the move, then to arrange for someone from Goodwill to come get donations, then to all the utility companies to turn off power and heat and cable television.

He signed papers, and ordered his favorite burger from his favorite Rocky Mountain café. He strolled the streets of downtown on Saturday night, and on Sunday morning, he drove into the mountains, back to the place where this new life had started.

He stayed in the car, though, unable to get out and face the cliffs that had altered his plans and put him on a different course.

"What do you wanna do, man?" the cabbie finally asked.

"Give me a few minutes, please." Sterling climbed from the car and headed down the trail that led to the ski cabin and lift. Though the beginning of May, a few mounds of snow remained. Mostly the ground was a sloppy, muddy mess, and Sterling stuck to the paved walkway.

He paused when the cabin came into view, as the towers holding the chairlifts broke through the trees. His eyes drifted closed, and he took a deep, deep drag of mountain-scented air. He felt the icy kiss of the winter wind against his cheeks. He smelled the fresh pines and the wax on his snowboard. Saw the shape of the snow, felt the ridges of his board catch in softer places and shoot forward in more frozen spots.

Sterling loved snowboarding. He knew with every cell in his body he'd do it again—and well. Relief and satisfaction combined in his core. He'd told his Burton rep and his Nordick rep that he'd be back on the slopes next winter. Maybe not competition worthy, he'd warned them.

But he hadn't known if what he'd said was true.

Here, now, in the shadow of the mountain that had swallowed him, he knew.

"Thank you, Lord," he whispered. "Thank you for everything that's happened after the fall."

Sterling turned his back on the mountain that had wrecked his life—and then given him a completely new one.

His whispered words of gratitude followed him back to his apartment, where he worked to finish everything he needed to before his flight left that evening. He didn't want to come back to Denver until next winter, when he was ready to show the world the new Sterling Maughan.

He hummed under his breath as he thought about Norah coming with him, standing beside him at all his press conferences, cheering for him from the stands as he did his run. In Sterling's fantasy, Javier was there too, and Erik and Alex.

Norah's mother remained a shadow in Sterling's mind,

someone he couldn't quite picture but couldn't ignore either.

His phone rang, forcing his fantasy into the recesses of his mind. "Hey, Rex." Sterling collapsed on the couch as his stomach roared. He'd worked through lunch.

"Hey."

Sterling didn't like the edge in his brother's voice, though he'd only spoken one word. The fact that he didn't continue meant Sterling wouldn't like the conversation.

"What's goin' on?" he asked, his heart doing a little tap dance in his chest.

"It's about Norah, Sterling."

CHAPTER 15

Sterling's ears turned deaf after Rex said the words, "She was a patient at Silver Creek, Sterling."

He'd stood up for Norah until then. Now he sat on the line, unlistening, as his brother continued to detail Norah's secrets.

Not lies. Sterling knew she'd never lied. She just hadn't given him the truth.

"I have to go," he blurted when Rex finally paused to take a breath. He didn't wait for his brother to confirm; Sterling simply hung up.

We looked it up, Sterling.

Unless you pay to have your name sealed, it's a public record.

She was there eleven years ago, Sterling.

Honestly, how well do you know her?

She was addicted to hydrocodone, Sterling.

Sterling groaned, bent forward, and put his palms over

his ears in an attempt to get Rex's accusations to silence. Sterling hadn't been able to say much during the call. A few "That's not true, Rex," and one "She would've told me," and "She's not like that," and the worst fuel he could've given Rex: "I love her."

Things and feelings that had gone dormant now surfaced. How dare Rex and his wife, Emily, "look into" Norah's past? What gave him that right? The anger directed at his brother quickly got redirected at Sterling.

Why hadn't he pressed her further about her family? About her past? About why she loved Silver Creek so much?

At the same time, why did it matter? Would he want someone judging him by who and what he'd done eleven years ago?

He shook his head, his emotions tangled and jumbled and knotted. He didn't even want Norah to know how ungodly he'd been six short months ago—but at least he'd been honest. He'd told her he'd stopped going to church, that he wasn't sure God had been there for him, all of it.

Because he trusted her.

He sat back as if someone had punched him. He trusted and loved her.

She claimed to love him, but she certainly didn't trust him. Not with the good, the bad, and the ugly of her life.

A sharp pain started in his chest, and he found it difficult to take a breath. He'd felt this way after he'd woken in the hospital too. Trapped. No way out. Alone. Hurt.

Phantom pain cascaded down his injured leg, and the muscles spasmed and jerked. He had to *get up, get out, go.*

Now, at least, he could. In the hospital, his leg had been attached to an apparatus in the ceiling. Here, he leapt from the couch and strode toward the door, his limp pronounced and sending pain through his whole body with every step.

He didn't care. He needed to get out into the open, free from the walls that echoed his brother's words back to him again and again.

———

Norah's somber mood matched Javier's as they sat through their second week of church without Sterling at their side. His absence seemed heavier this week, almost like a physical presence she couldn't shake.

With ten minutes left in the service, she got up to leave. "Meet you in the car," she whispered to Javier. "Bring the littles out when it's over."

He looked like he wanted to go with her right then, but she shook her head. She needed some time alone—though she'd had plenty of that this weekend. She'd breezed through her other cabins in the mountains, and sat outside Six Sons, wishing she could go in and find her peace in the bunk bed room.

But half a dozen cars had littered the driveway; Nancy's important client had obviously brought friends. Norah would go up on Tuesday evening to clean up after them, just to give them an extra day if they decided not to leave this afternoon, as scheduled.

Norah's heels clicked on the wood floor of the lobby as she

escaped the church. A set of footsteps and Dr. Richards saying, "Norah, wait," made her pause before exiting the building.

She took a deep breath to stuff the threatening tears back where they belonged: out of sight.

"Doctor Richards?" She turned toward him, unsure as to when she'd spoken to him so much outside of work.

"Are you heading out?" he asked, his wise eyes searching hers. "I need to speak with you, privately."

Her nerves pulsed out a jolt of fear, and Norah almost bolted. "I was just going to wait in the car for my brothers."

He cocked his head to the side. "Not enjoying the sermon?"

Norah rubbed the back of her neck. "Having a hard time concentrating today."

Dr. Richards opened the church door and gestured for her to go in front of him. "I'll make this quick." He walked next to her as they circled the church. The weather was cooperating, for now.

"Norah, I'm concerned about your relationship with Sterling Maughan."

Norah's feet froze along with her internal organs. She tired to say something, but nothing made it past her iced lungs.

"I saw you two at the grocery store last night. Shopping. One cart. You obviously followed him up the mountain to his house." He held up his hands. "I'm not saying anything inappropriate is going on, but well, I've got eyes. I know you like him."

"I love him." Norah's vocal chords thawed with the words. "I'm sorry, Doctor Richards. I know there's a policy at Silver Creek and all, but we'd started dating before he started working there, and I kept telling him we needed to talk to you, that you're reasonable, but he doesn't think the policy means anything. He's never really thought he'd lose his job over it."

Her words rushed and tripped and fought against each other. "I can't lose my job," Norah blurted. But she couldn't lose Sterling either. She bit down on those words.

"And I know you need Sterling." She waited, hoping and praying with everything she had that Dr. Richards wouldn't fire her. Not here. Not at church. Not when she was trying to do the right thing by being at church when she really wanted to nap.

"I do need Sterling." Dr. Richards sighed and looked up to the mountains where Sterling lived, as if he could see him there. "And I need you, too."

Norah didn't dare hope, didn't dare to speak.

"I suppose a policy can be changed," he said.

"Sterling will probably quit in the fall anyway," Norah said. For some reason she couldn't name, her voice trembled. "He's re-joining the snowboarding circuit next winter. He'll need to start training."

Dr. Richards studied her. "Maybe you two can keep your relationship under wraps until then? Do you think anyone else knows about you two?"

Norah shrugged, more and more tremors wracking her

body. She couldn't understand her reaction—she should be happy Dr. Richards hadn't fired her on the spot.

"I doubt it," Norah said. "I haven't told anyone, and I don't think Sterling has either."

"Maybe we just keep it a secret for now."

"A secret?" Norah smiled at him. "I didn't think those were allowed at Silver Creek either."

"Well, I am the boss." Dr. Richards flashed a rare smile that lasted less than two seconds. "So it's not really a secret if I know about it, is it?"

"If you say so." Norah grinned at him and managed to make it to her car just as the first patrons exited the church.

Feeling like she wanted to cry, but unsure as to why, Norah dropped her brothers off at home and drove around Gold Valley. The urge to turn and head up the mountain grew to unavoidable levels.

Still, Norah kept the car in the valley. She drove past the elementary school where she'd attended for six years. She admired the stillness of Main Street in the late afternoon: the bank, the chocolate shop, the movie theater, the pharmacy, and the dog spa all lined up. Across from them sat the cupcake eatery, the dry cleaners, the salon, and the best pizza joint Norah had ever eaten at. She hadn't been surprised to see Luigi's boxes when she'd first discovered Sterling in the basement.

She maneuvered through the town in a circular radius, noting where the post office was, and her favored childhood park. She entered the new development—or what would be the new development—where she and Sterling would look at the two available models the next evening.

Now, a few early homes existed, as well as cement curbs and leveled dirt for roads. The model home shone as dusk fell, and finally Norah gave in to her desire to go to the cabin.

When she arrived, the driveway and garage sat empty, so she pulled in like she normally did. She entertained the idea of grabbing her bucket of cleaning supplies from the shelf in the garage as she entered. In the end, she left them where they were, not wanting to do today what wasn't expected of her until Tuesday.

She entered the sleeping house, and became instantly aware of the activities that had taken place over the weekend. Pizza boxes and takeout containers sat stacked in the too-small trashcan. Soda cans and water bottles littered the counter. Blankets lay in heaps in the living room, and blinds had been left open for all to see.

Norah didn't care. She'd bill Nancy for the extra hours it took to haul out trash and re-organize everything. And Nancy would pay. She always had; never questioned.

With every step up to the bunk bed room, Norah's spirits lifted. She didn't dare cross over to the master bedroom—it wasn't her goal anyway. She entered the room and sat on her bunk bed to watch the sky swallow the sun.

As the radiant beams of light turned from gold to crimson to blue, Norah thought about Sterling. With a start, she realized he should've called already. Called to say he was boarding and would be home soon. Called to find out if he

could come home to the cabin or if he needed to find somewhere to crash that night.

He'd wanted it to be at her house.

She'd distracted him with a declaration of her love. Even
if it was true, she shouldn't have used her affection to deter
him from coming to her house. Sharp guilt pulled against
her stomach, tore holes through her conscience.

Why had she done that?

She tipped her head back, and asked God. "Why do I do
that?"

He didn't answer, at least not in verbal words Norah
heard in her ears. But she felt something prick her mind,
touch her heart.

She needed to trust Sterling.

"How?" she begged the Lord. But no feeling came, and
Norah clutched her knees to her chest as she searched her
brain for an answer she didn't have.

———

Norah waited at the cabin until the edge of night. She
rationalized that Sterling had simply forgotten to call. She'd
looked up his flight, and it was on-time, due to arrive in
Missoula in twenty minutes.

"What are *you* doing here?"

Norah swung her attention from the dark horizon
outside the window to the woman standing in the doorway
of the bunk bed room. She stalked a step closer, her expression dangerous. "You shouldn't be here."

Adrenaline urged Norah to stay, hold her ground. "I was just waiting for Sterling."

"He doesn't want to see you anymore." The woman cocked her hip and placed a perfectly manicured hand on it. She screamed money, from the color of her bottle-blonde hair to the gold sandals she wore.

Norah blinked at her. "I'm sorry, ma'am. But who are you?"

"I'm Emily Maughan."

Emily, Emily. Norah racked her brain to figure out which one of the brothers had married an Emily. She couldn't come up with an answer before the woman added, "Rex's wife."

Not wanting a repeat of the emotional turmoil she'd endured when Rex had said "the help," Norah scooted to the edge of the bed and stood. "I'm sorry. I'll go."

"That's right you will. And you won't come back."

Norah paused next to her. Though the woman stood only an inch or two shorter than Norah, Norah felt as small as an ant. Smaller even, from the glare Emily gave her. "I'll be back on Tuesday to clean up."

Emily sniffed. "That won't be necessary. I'm sending a cleaning lady."

"But I'm—"

"Fired," Emily said. "I've already spoken to Nancy about your…inappropriate advances toward Sterling. She authorized me to fire you."

A cold hand reached into Norah's chest, wrapped its icy fingers around her heart, and squeezed. Squeezed tight.

"Sterling is staying in Denver," Emily continued, as if she had no idea how her words had strangled Norah. "We told him everything about you, Norah Watson." Her eyes burned with repressed anger as she sneered out Norah's name. "You should've told him everything. He's devastated. Claims to love you and everything."

She crowded Norah's space. "He doesn't deserve someone like you hurting him. He's been through enough. Rex and I have sworn to protect him, help him. So you should leave. And you shouldn't come back." She stepped back, her speech delivered, and with enough fury to rival a hurricane.

Norah didn't know what to do. "Sterling's staying in Denver?"

"That's right. He had a good life there, and he can be happy there again." Emily pointed to the door. "Go on, now. If we find out you've even stepped one foot inside this cabin again, we'll call the police."

Horrified and dumbstruck, and with little option, Norah moved past her and flew down the stairs. She dashed into the garage, put the key in the ignition with shaking hands, and drove down the mountain with tears staining her face.

CHAPTER 16

Tell me you're coming back to Montana.

Sterling stared at Norah's text, the letters burning into his retina. He really needed to return to Gold Valley, but he'd already missed the last flight out. He'd called and spoken to Dr. Richards, who'd reassured him he could return to work on Tuesday.

That only gave him one day—twenty-four hours—to figure out what to do about Norah. He couldn't fathom what Rex had told her, but it was obviously something about him staying in Denver.

New fury roared to life inside his chest. He hadn't told Rex he was staying in Denver. He'd simply been too numb, and too confused, and too wounded to make it to the airport. He hadn't even gone back to the apartment yet.

"Anything else, hon?" The waitress stood next to his table, coffee pot in hand. He'd downed at least a half-dozen cups, ordered and eaten dinner and then dessert.

"What time do you close?" he asked.

"About an hour." She refreshed his coffee. "I'll get you the bill now. Stay as long as you like."

He hadn't been able to get himself to get up and go, exactly the way he hadn't been motivated to do more than lie in a nest of blankets at the cabin. Until Norah. Once he'd met her, everything had changed.

In only eight short weeks, he'd gotten up, gotten back behind the wheel, gotten on a horse, gotten a job, gotten back on good terms with God, gotten on with his life.

I'm coming home tomorrow, he typed out. When he sent the message to Norah, a weight lifted from his shoulders. *Just missed my flight.*

He hesitated. He didn't just want to sweep what he'd learned about her under the rug. He wanted to dig at it until he heard the whole truth from her beautiful lips. But he didn't want to ask, didn't want to show up with rakes and shovels and pitchforks when she didn't want to volunteer information.

She didn't respond, and Sterling paid his bill before trudging down the block to his boxed-up apartment.

Don't ask, he coached himself as he tossed and turned that night. *She should come to you.*

By five-thirty in the morning, Sterling felt stretched thin. His flight wasn't until mid-afternoon, and he typed out at least ten texts, all of them asking Norah to come pick him up at the airport. But it was a long drive, and he'd parked in the economy lot, and she couldn't afford to come that far just to appease him.

Sterling paused as he sat up in bed. He should've known more about Norah than he did. She always took his gas money, though it was obviously a lot more than it cost her to fill her tank. She'd only argued with him about it once.

She never invited him to her house, but Sterling knew the address. He'd sent food to Javier, Erik, and Alex enough times to have it memorized. He'd never considered driving by just to see where she lived.

He hadn't cared.

He still didn't.

But *Norah* obviously did, and Sterling had missed the signs. Sorrow replaced the simmering hurt beneath his ribs. Still, she didn't trust him with the knowledge about her heritage, where she came from, whether it was a one-bedroom house in the worst neighborhood in town or a fancy high-rise apartment.

"No, that's all you," he told himself as he headed for the shower, all thoughts of going back to sleep gone now. And Norah knew all about his apartment in Denver and his massive, three-story cabin in the gated mountain community.

But Sterling couldn't change who he was. He couldn't change who his parents were, just like she couldn't. He looked at himself in the mirror, and for the first time in a long time, he liked who he saw looking back.

He wasn't perfect, but he was more righteous than he'd been before. He wasn't perfect, but he was kinder and more sensitive than he'd been before. He wasn't perfect, but he worked hard—and wanted to work harder than he had before. At snowboarding. At his relationship with God. At living his life.

At being with Norah? The thought flew into his mind, unbidden but present nonetheless. He turned away from his reflection, unsure of how to answer the question.

———

A knock sounded on his door as he finished shaving. The clock inset into the mirror read six-twelve. He splashed aftershave on his face, unconcerned about getting the door. Surely he'd heard wrong. The neighbor's pipes or something. Someone couldn't even get in the building without a code.

He pulled on gym shorts and a T-shirt before zipping up his bag. The knock sounded again, louder this time. Only a few seconds passed before the doorbell rang.

Perplexed, Sterling left his bag on his bed and entered the living room like he expected to see a cat burglar cracking the safe behind the artwork. The remaining echo of the bell faded into silence.

Another knock, more persistent now. Sterling moved to the door quickly now, not wanting the knocking and doorbell ringing to wake his neighbors. He paused to check through the peephole and jerked back, sure his eyes were playing tricks on him.

Because Norah stood in the hall.

He looked again.

Norah stood in the hall, wringing her hands and

glancing around her. She turned back to the door and raised her fist to knock again.

Sterling pulled open the door, his heart pounding in his ears and making his throat narrow.

She flinched away from him, those slender fingers working around and around themselves.

"How did you get here?" he asked. "What are you doing here?" He was supremely glad he'd ignored her first knock and put on some clothes instead. "It's six-fifteen in the morning."

"I came straight from the airport." She hooked her thumb over her shoulder. "Did you know your building is almost impossible to get into?"

Sterling folded his arms, though he wanted to wrap them around Norah and hold on tight. "I did know that. It's one of its best perks." He peered at her. "How did you get in?"

"I called your mother, and she gave me the code." Norah didn't smile. Didn't laugh. But Sterling didn't believe for one moment that his mother gave her the code. In the middle of the night? No way.

"Norah—"

"She also said she didn't authorize your sister-in-law to fire me." Norah's eyes shot angry fire, but Sterling suspected it wasn't meant for him.

"Emily fired you?"

Norah's jaw worked as her fingers stilled. "Can I come in?" She glanced toward the neighbor's door several yards down the hall.

Sterling stepped back, the possibility of being shut into his apartment with Norah appealing to him in an odd way. He resisted the urge to swoop in and kiss her, reassure her everything was fine, that he still loved her.

"Did you really call my mother?"

"I really did." Norah's gaze swept the apartment, and Sterling wished his kitchen counter bore a couple of scratches or a deep dent. Something.

"Norah," he tried again.

She turned toward him, her eyes soft now, and her chin held high. "I came to talk," she said. "There's a lot I need to say."

"I've got time." He moved past the small table to the right of the kitchen and into his living room. He'd stacked boxes against one wall, but the sofa and the chair were still usable. He chose the chair so she wouldn't be able to reject him by not sitting next to him on the couch.

She sat too, right on the edge of the couch and set her purse on the floor. Tucking an errant curl behind her ear— an action Sterling had done on countless occasions, and one he wanted to do again—she took a deep breath.

"Your mother doesn't approve of our relationship," she started. "But she did agree to help me get here to see you, because I begged her and told her it was the only way to help you."

"And what do I need help with, Norah?" He kept his gaze on the floor, because looking at her was too painful. He also thought she'd be able to speak easier if he wasn't watching her with the intensity he felt blowing through his veins.

"I don't know, Sterling. But I need to set things right between us. And I don't know who told you what, but I do know that your brother's wife showed up at the cabin, told me I was fired, and that you were staying in Denver." She wiped her palms on her knees. "So I came to Denver."

Sterling wanted to rage at her for not telling him everything in Montana. Wanted to grin at her and give her one of his lazy smirks to let her know he understood. Wanted to kiss her and make her mixed up life better.

"I came to Denver to tell you I love you. And I came to tell you that it terrifies me to my very core to have you meet my mother."

His eyes shot up to meet hers. "I want to meet her."

"She is…unkind. She will not be nice to you. She won't even try."

"Have you told her about me?"

Norah's right leg began to bounce. "No."

Sterling couldn't fault her. He hadn't exactly mentioned her to anyone in his family. "Norah, I want to meet her. I don't care if she's nice to me or not. *You're* nice to me, and that's all that matters."

Her eyes turned glassy and she swiped one hand across her face. "You're going to miss your real estate appointments tonight."

"I don't care," Sterling said.

"I'll take you home to meet her tonight, if you want. What time is your flight?"

"Early enough to meet your mother for dinner."

Norah shook her head. "She doesn't leave the house."

"Your house, then." Sterling watched her carefully in an attempt to confirm his suspicions. Sure enough, her throat tightened and she could barely swallow.

"The first time we met, I made a vow with myself that you would never see my house."

Sterling chuckled; he couldn't help it. "Norah, how did you think that possible?"

She shrugged. "It was the first time we met."

"Oh, Norah." His voice turned low and deep. "I knew the first time I met you that we'd end up together."

She blinked at him, blinked some more. "I'll work on believing that. Because I came to tell you that I'm still struggling to believe that someone like you would want to be with someone like me."

Someone like me. The words reverberated through his head and down into his chest. He got up and moved to sit next to her on the couch. "Norah, I don't know who you think you are. But when I look at you, I see a woman so kind, so hardworking, so caring. I see someone I want to share everything with, who I can't wait to get alone so I can kiss her, someone who has always put everyone before herself. And I want to change that. I want to take care of you."

Tears splashed her cheeks. "I came to Denver to tell you that the first time I went to Silver Creek, it was as a fifteen-year-old. I was a patient for twelve weeks after one of Mama's boyfriends introduced me to pain medication." Her voice hollowed with every word, and she stared at an unknown spot on the wall across from them. "I started taking them at first because I had migraines. Then I realized I could escape my life if I took more. So I did."

Sterling's heart cracked for her, for the kind of life she'd had to endure, for the pain and endless string of bad luck.

"I don't care about what's in the past," he said. "Heaven knows I'm not perfect."

She half giggled, half sobbed. "You sure seem to be."

"Don't tell me you've forgotten the nest you found me in." He lifted his arm and placed it around her shoulders, gently bringing her into his chest. "And Norah, I'm not gonna lie. It's been real hard for me to leave Denver. Real hard. I actually wondered if you were worth it."

She stiffened, but he forged on. "I love snowboarding, Norah. I love it. When I thought I'd never be able to do it again, it wrecked me. And then I met you, and I realized there was more to life than snowboarding. And then when I found out I could have both? I didn't know what to do. It seemed like I couldn't have both, at least not at the same time."

He pressed a kiss to her forehead, her cheek, slowly working his way to her mouth. "But then everything started slipping into place. My apartment sold quickly. My sponsorships have been renewed. Gordon doesn't care where I train, as long as I do. It seemed as if God himself was saying, 'Sterling, you better stay in Gold Valley and somehow get that Norah Watson to stay with you.'"

He kissed her, slowly urging her to go with him deeper and longer than before. When she finally pulled back, he pressed his face into the crook of her neck. "I'm in love with you, Norah Watson, and I don't care if my mother doesn't approve, or about what happened ten years ago, or what my brother's wife says. I just want to be with you."

A few seconds of silence drew a blip of unease into his mind.

"I came here to talk," she said, her voice barely crossing the distance between them. "And you said all the right things." She lightly punched his arm. "It's not fair."

"You'll get better at telling me things," Sterling said. "After all, I'm going to push you to do it everyday."

Norah groaned even as she snuggled further into him.

Norah flew back to Great Falls alone—she'd left her car there, and she didn't want Sterling to have to make a four-hour drive after landing in Missoula.

She'd tried to get a flight out of the same airport as him, but they didn't have anything until the morning. And that wasn't acceptable to her.

Apparently, charging an expensive, last-minute flight out of an airport she'd never been to was acceptable to her. Seeing Sterling's face had been worth it. Seeing the acceptance in his eyes, even though he stood with his arms crossed and that adorable frown between his eyes, had been worth ten airplane tickets. Having him tell her he knew they'd end up together from the first time they met meant the world to her.

Once he'd learned she wouldn't be able to fly home with him, he'd suggested they postpone meeting her mom until the next night. So Norah drove through the National Forest with the radio silent, her thoughts the only chorus she needed.

She pulled into Gold Valley just as the sun dipped below the horizon. She'd promised phone calls to a few people. Dr. Richards received the first one, and Norah assured him she'd made it to Denver and back in one piece and that she'd be at work in the morning.

"Thank you so much." Norah's throat closed.

"Norah, you haven't taken a day off in five years," he said. "Did Sterling make it back?"

She coached herself to breathe through the emotion. She needed to learn how to speak when she didn't want to—Sterling had said he'd push her to do just that. Funnily enough, for him, she *wanted* to do that.

"His flight was an hour after mine," she said. "But he should be on the road home by now."

"I'll see you both tomorrow." He paused, and Norah waited because she had enough experience to know that Dr. Richards hadn't said all he wanted to. "And Norah, I've never seen you so happy. So whatever happened that sent you to Denver in the middle of the night, it's probably worth fixing."

That blasted lump in Norah's throat made her voice thick when she said, "You're right, Doctor Richards. I'm trying."

"Norah, I think it's time you started calling me Len." He laughed and she joined in, quickly sobering when he added, "After all, you're not even close to the fifteen-year-old I first met."

She agreed and hung up, but his words refused to leave her mind. She wasn't the fifteen-year-old she'd been when she first met Dr. Richards. She'd worked hard to leave that life, that person, behind. She'd done it.

But how often did that person, those choices, still haunt her?

All the time.

Not anymore, she sternly told herself as she dialed Lori. "Not anymore," she said out loud as the line rang.

Norah explained everything to Javier, who sat with her in the living room while the littler boys slept on the floor in front of them. Their world had been turned upside down, and Norah had only been gone for one day.

"I'm worried," she told her brother while she waited for Sterling to call. "What will happen to you guys when I leave?" At least she'd stopped saying "if." She knew now she'd be leaving this house, this life, behind. She didn't know what would happen, or when, or where she'd end up, but she now knew she wasn't confined to Gold Valley, wasn't chained to Mama.

Mama, who hadn't even known she'd left town in the middle of the night. Mama, who had squinted at her when Norah had mentioned meeting Sterling the following evening. Mama, who Norah was starting to break away from.

"Norah," Javier said quietly so he wouldn't wake the boys. "We rely on you a lot. Too much. If you weren't here, things would be fine. Maybe Mama would come out of her room."

She nodded. Intellectually, she knew Javier was right. Emotionally, though, she couldn't fathom moving out of the house at the same time Javier did. And he deserved to go to college.

"We could break up at any time," she said.

Javier chuckled. "Norah, I've seen him talk about you. He's not letting you go. So if you want to break up, that's all on you."

Warmth akin to the heat from the sun filled her. "You think so?"

"I know so."

Her phone rang, effectively silencing her protest. "It's Sterling."

"Tell him hi for me." Javier grinned at her. "I can't believe you're dating *the* Sterling Maughan."

She returned his smile. "Don't let him hear you call him that. He doesn't like it."

"He doesn't?" The panic in her brother's voice was almost comical.

Norah stood and strode away from him as she answered. "Hey."

"Hey, beautiful." He wore his emotion in his voice.

"You sound happy."

"I am."

"Oh, yeah? Good news on the flight home?"

"Not really."

She imagined him leaning against the doorframe, phone held casually to his ear as he tried to pretend like he didn't have a care in the world.

"You free for a few minutes?"

She spun toward the front of the house, but darkness bathed the window. "Ye-es." She drew out the word as she tried to tame her pulse. Was he here? Now?

"I'm standing out front. Want to show you something."

Norah took the deepest breath she could manage with lungs that felt encased in quicksand. "You could come in, if you wanted." She added a shrug to her statement, though he surely couldn't see through the grimy window. "Javier would like to say hello, I'm sure."

Sure enough, behind her, Javier said, "Is that Sterling? Is he here?"

"He's out front," she said to him. "Come on in," she told Sterling, while she tried to tell herself that the idea wasn't completely ridiculous.

She hung up as her brother leapt from the couch and opened the front door they barely used. It squealed on its hinges, and Norah cringed. What if Mama heard it and started yelling at them to keep it down?

But neither Erik nor Alex even moved, and they lay only a few feet from the door. Sterling's impressive height and shoulders filled the doorway, causing Norah's breath to catch in her chest. She wondered if he'd always affect her in such a way, and as she smiled at him from behind Javier's back, she hoped so.

"Hey," he said to Javier as he squeezed past him and into the house. "You guys got anything to drink? I drove straight here from the airport, and I'm parched."

"Sure." Javier went into the kitchen and grabbed a bottle

of water from the fridge. Norah stood marveling at Sterling, who didn't assess the peeling wallpaper, the carpet in desperate need of a cleaner, the somewhat stale scent Norah knew hung in the air.

He stepped up to her, drew her into an embrace, and kissed her forehead. Then he moved away and sat on their threadbare couch just as Javier handed him the water bottle. "Thanks, man." He beamed up at her brother like he'd just presented him with a briefcase containing a million dollars.

All of Norah's fears evaporated, right there in her brightly lit living room, with its mismatched lamps and crooked picture frames and a pair of dirty boys sleeping on the floor. Her heart swelled with love for the man who didn't judge her based on her square footage.

"Thank you," she whispered as she sank onto the sofa next to him.

"Love you." He slid his arm over her shoulders and pulled her into his side, his adoration and attention on her now. For the first time in her life, Norah felt worthy of such affections.

———

Sterling ignored the buzzing in his pocket, knowing it would be his mother. He'd called her while he waited for his flight in Denver, but the time difference had proven difficult for getting in touch with her. How Norah had managed it, he wasn't sure. Maybe it had been an act of God. A true miracle.

Now, though, sitting on Norah's couch while she dozed against his chest, he wasn't going to answer. He'd call her on the way up the mountain, because he was sure he wouldn't like what she had to say.

Still, Norah was being brave about him meeting her mom, and Sterling owed it to her to talk to his parents. He should probably send an email to his nosy brothers too. Rex had already gotten an earful—Sterling had called him as soon as Norah had boarded her plane.

With lots of apologies and reassurances that he and Emily would mind their own business, Sterling had then set his sights on his parents.

"I should go." He fought against a yawn and lost. "I have to work in the morning."

"Mm." Norah snugged deeper against him, and he wanted this reality to become permanent. He wondered what a full life with her would hold, and a smile formed on his face.

"Come on, sleepyhead. You need to get to bed too." She'd napped in his apartment that morning, but she'd been up all night, and a couple of hours on his couch wouldn't cut it. "Javier's already got the other boys down the hall."

She sat up and covered her eyes with her hand. "All right. I'll walk you out." She stood and stretched, the hem of her T-shirt lifting slightly above her waistband. Her delicious, dark skin called to him, and he swallowed.

After moving around the couch, she flipped a light switch and turned toward him. "See you tomorrow." She pressed her palms against his chest and leaned into him for a kiss. He obliged, a rush of electricity sparking through his chest.

He ducked out the doorway, aware of Norah's eyes on his back as he crossed the lawn to his truck. His boots bore the remnants of winter, and he cranked the heater once he'd started the engine. He drove away, his mind simultaneously whirring and withering from exhaustion.

Tapping his screen, he dialed his mother. She answered on the second ring. "Mom."

"Sterling."

She wouldn't start the necessary conversation. She never did. "So I heard my girlfriend called you."

"Nice to know you have a girlfriend."

Sterling chuckled. "We hadn't exactly talked about labels yet, Mom. It's no big deal."

"The girl flew to Denver to see you."

Out of desperation, Sterling thought, the familiar taste of bitterness on the back of his tongue. He swallowed. No, she hadn't told him everything, but that didn't mean she wasn't planning to. His meddling brother had just beat her to it.

"Thanks for giving her the code to get in the building." He turned and went across the railroad tracks, his headlights cutting swathes of light through the dark neighborhood. "My apartment sold really quickly. I need something here."

"You'll find something. So you think you like Norah?" Her voice strayed into the *you-don't-have-to-tell-me-but-you-really-do* range.

Sterling took his time answering. He did like Norah. Her

house had been about what he'd expected, but only because he'd spent ten minutes in the parking garage at the airport on Google Maps, looking at it. If he hadn't done that, he might have been more shocked. He wasn't sure. And he didn't know how to feel about it. Should he be upset at himself for being shallow? Should he beat himself up for having somewhere nice to live?

"Sterling?"

"Yeah, Mom. I like Norah." He wanted to tell his mother that he'd actually fallen in love with Norah, but he bit the words back.

"How much do you like Norah?"

"Mom." He sighed and eased the truck onto the main road that would lead him past Silver Creek and up the mountain.

"What? I'm just trying to figure out if there will be a wedding soon."

Sterling laughed. Tossed his head back and guffawed. "No, Mom. But one day."

The lengthy pause on the other end of the line told him she hadn't been expecting that.

"Really? You're going to marry her?"

"As soon as she's ready." Sterling saw a light on in the cabin where his boys lived, and his heart jumped over one of its beats. Who was up? What did they need?

He forced the worries away when his mother said, "Well, I don't know how I feel about that."

"Doesn't matter how you feel about it," Sterling said, a

hint of ice in his tone. "I love her, and we're gonna get married one day."

Deal with it, he added silently.

"She's a nice woman, Mom. Goes to church every week. Takes care of her brothers and her mom. Works two jobs, and goes to school at night." He couldn't see why his mother wouldn't approve of her. Maybe what Rex had said had been wrong.

"I know all about Norah Watson." The volume on the line halved. Or had she just spoken quieter?

"I know you do, Mom. She's worked for you for years, so you know how reliable, honest, and godly she is."

"Yes, I do."

"Tell Rex, would you?" Sterling asked as he maneuvered around the curves of the mountain. "I have to go, all right? I'll call you later."

She said her good-byes, and Sterling hung up. By the time he got to the cabin, exhaustion was winning over everything else. He towed his luggage inside, made it down the spiral staircase without dying, and collapsed in bed.

CHAPTER 18

"He'll be here in about five minutes, Mama." Norah couldn't sit. She paced from the living room to the kitchen and back, about five steps. She'd told Mama about Sterling last night, after he'd left. Again this morning. For a third time when she got home from work.

She'd been scrubbing surfaces for the past two hours, though Sterling had already been inside the house. Javier came down the hall, spraying continuously with the air freshener. "Bathroom's done."

Norah flashed him a grateful look, but couldn't seem to articulate anything. *Please let her be nice,* she prayed. *Just this once, let her be nice.*

Norah had never brought anyone home to meet Mama. Everyone in town knew it. She didn't even know how things like this normally went.

The timer in the kitchen went off, and Norah jumped

from the shrill beep. She spun and hurried back the way she'd come, snatching the oven mitts from the counter where she'd left them. She pulled out the once-frozen lasagna and put in the waiting garlic bread.

A knock sounded on the door.

She froze.

Her heart raced.

Mama swung her head in Norah's direction. At least she'd showered that day. And Norah had insisted she get dressed. Thankfully, Mama had complied.

Norah wondered what the price would be.

Javier opened the door, moving time forward again and unfreezing Norah's feet. "Hey, man." He grabbed Sterling's hand and they patted each other on the back. "Come on in."

Norah made it to the spot where the carpet met the linoleum, her fingers twining and untwining. "Hey," she said.

"Hey yourself." He strode toward her and embraced her. "You look great. Don't worry so much." His whispered words in her ear brought her little comfort.

He stepped back and turned toward Mama. "Mama, this is Sterling Maughan."

Recognition lit her mother's face. She released the dark ends of her hair, which she'd been playing with. "Sterling Maughan. Nice to meet you."

Every muscle in Norah's body sighed in relief. Mama was going to be nice.

"Come sit over here," she said, gesturing to the couch.

Sterling laced his fingers through hers and brought

Norah with him. "Nice to meet you too, ma'am." His cowboy accent slipped out, and Norah grinned.

"Tell me all about that Amber Lyons. She sure was a pretty thing. Saw her on the TV a time or two."

Norah couldn't suppress the groan fast enough, and it slipped between her lips. Thankfully, Javier called, "Bread's done. Let's eat," before Sterling could bolt.

———

A week later, she stood against the fence separating her from a large yard, watching him ride a much bigger horse. Owen's new one, Pompeii. Sterling was doing just fine, like he did with most things. They'd gone to look at floor plans in the new development on the north edge of town, and he'd chosen one. He wouldn't tell her if he'd bought the two-story model or the more Montanan rancher-style. He said it would be a "surprise."

She was just glad he thought she'd still be around come winter.

Stop it, she told herself. Sterling showered love and adoration on her. On Saturday, she'd entered the cabin to find two dozen red roses waiting for her on the main level kitchen counter. Sunday after church, he'd taken her brothers to the movies so she could sleep.

And still, she doubted he could keep up this behavior for much longer. That he even wanted to. For her.

Not for her.

Maybe for someone like Amber.

Familiar melancholy descended on her, and when she caught Sterling's eye, she indicated she'd see him later. He waved, and she left. With dinner on the table and Mama tucked safely in her bedroom, Norah finished her homework while she waited for Sterling to show up. Since he'd met Mama, he'd been coming to her house after work. It worked better for her to feed her brothers and complete classwork. He kept longer hours than her, but he never complained about sitting on her couch until late at night, the thirty-minute drive up the mountain, or the early hours at Silver Creek.

On the phone with my mother. Might be late.

Sterling's text made Norah's blood cool. He hadn't said anything about his mother since Denver, and though Norah had emailed and texted a *thank you* to Nancy for the building codes, she hadn't gotten a response either.

How are you texting while talking to your mother? While she considered him capable of all things, even he couldn't text and talk at the same time.

She's talking, he sent. *I'm supposed to be listening.*

What is she saying?

Something about not starting snowboarding too soon.

I agree with her.

Sterling didn't text after that, and he didn't show up until almost nine o'clock. By then, Norah's eyelids felt like someone had tied bricks to them.

"Sorry," he said as he entered the kitchen from the garage. "Everyone's in bed?"

"Finals for Javier tomorrow," she said. "Field day for the others. I sent them to bed early."

He slid his hands along her waist, bringing her flush against him. "Missed you today."

"Did you?" Why couldn't she believe him when he said such sweet things?

He stepped back, obviously having heard something in her tone she hadn't been able to mask. "Norah."

She didn't like it when he said her name like that. The vein of frustration along the edges made the snakes in her stomach riot.

"You hungry or did you stop somewhere?"

"Not hungry."

She turned toward the kitchen anyway. Sterling would eat if she got the food out. She pulled the broccoli salad out of the fridge and reached for the package of hot dogs.

"Why do you do that?" he asked.

"Do what?" She stuck a couple of hot dogs in the microwave.

"When are you going to start to believe that I care about you?"

"I know you care about me." With nothing left to do, she faced him.

"You know." He gazed right at her, those dark eyes probing for the truth. If she didn't look away, he'd find it. "But you don't believe it."

She sighed. "That's not true—"

"It *is* true." He glanced away, down the hall as if checking to see if Javier loitered there. He often did, wanting to say hello to his idol. "I'm tired, Norah. I'm gonna head home."

"Tired?"

"Yeah." He ignored the food she'd gotten out and fished his keys out of his jeans pocket. "Tired of trying to prove to you that I love you. It's so exhausting."

She wasn't sure how to respond. Her mind spun with what he'd said, rearranging the words into more damaging patterns.

"Here's the deal. I love you, but at some point I'm going to disappoint you. I'm not going to do enough, or maybe I've done too much. Set the bar too high. I don't know." He smashed his cowboy hat back on his head, effectively concealing his eyes. "What I do know is you need to make a decision. Either figure out how to believe I want to be with you, or break up with me."

"Break up—" The idea horrified Norah, but his statement punched her right where her pulse pounded. "I don't want to break up."

"Good." Sterling swept his lips across her cheek, lingering near her ear lobe. "But you really do need to figure out how to believe me."

Her bones felt like tofu. "I'm trying."

He didn't say anything, only removed his hands from her body and slipped out the door. He hadn't said it, but Norah had heard, *Try harder.*

———

Sterling woke to his alarm at five a.m. and stayed in bed for a few extra minutes. Then he heaved himself from the warmth of his blankets and headed into the game room, where he'd set up free weights. His new morning routine: Getting back in shape.

He couldn't run, but he could lift. His leg ached after a morning weight training session, and horseback riding didn't help. But Sterling took painkillers and worked through the discomfort. Determination drove him. Determination to be on the slopes come winter, and that meant his leg needed to be strong.

A couple of weeks had passed, and while Norah still let him kiss her, he didn't go to her house every night after work like he'd been doing. He probably shouldn't have given her an ultimatum, but trying to think of ways to prove his love to her had kept him awake at night. He didn't think being in love should be so hard.

Now, snowboarding filled his dreams at night, almost taunting him since it was almost Independence Day, and though the highest peaks in Montana still boasted some snow, it wasn't nearly enough to board with.

After work, he usually drove to the rec center to swim—his preferred method of working out in the summer. Low resistance and relief from the heat helped. He hadn't told Norah, but he'd ordered a swimming pool for his backyard. He wasn't going to tell anyone, actually. Normal people in Montana didn't install pools in their backyards. The idea was pretty ridiculous.

He sighed as he hung his cowboy hat in his locker,

followed by his boots and jeans. Gliding through the cool water brought him more than just a few hundred calories burned. The relief from the sun and wind of the Montana stables would've been enough to lure Sterling to the pool every afternoon.

You should call and cancel the pool, he told himself. *After all, next summer, you won't be at Silver Creek.*

He'd already told Dr. Richards he'd only be around for one more group of boys. Thirteen more weeks. Dr. Richards had asked him to reconsider, but Sterling didn't exactly need the money and he'd rather spend his time working out, conditioning, and then snowboarding once the weather cooperated in the fall.

Sterling hadn't told Norah yet. As he dove into the pool, he wondered if Dr. Richards had. His powerful strokes cut through the water, and he pushed himself to go faster, flip quicker, in an attempt to drive Norah from his mind.

Didn't work.

———

Norah stalked Sterling for almost three weeks before she followed him into the recreation center. She'd never actually been inside. Sure, they hosted programs for kids Erik and Alex would've liked, but Norah didn't have the extra funds for soccer or swimming.

Each evening, Sterling carried a duffle bag into the center. She wasn't sure what he did inside, and today she was determined to find out.

And to tell him she needed him back in her life full-time. This part-time, walking-on-eggshell type of relationship wasn't really working for her.

Him, either, if the dark circles under his eyes indicated anything. The drawn down shape of his mouth. The tension in his shoulders whenever they were together.

"Miss?" the attendant called after her as she passed the desk.

Norah half-turned back to her, trying not to lose sight of Sterling. "Hmm?"

"Do you have a pass?"

No, Norah did not have a pass. "Oh, I'm—I just need to catch my friend." Her voice stalled, for more than one reason. Number one, Sterling had surpassed the friend label long ago, and it sounded false calling him that. Number two, she didn't actually want him to see her yet. Not until she knew what he did here and could order the appropriate words to say to him.

She glanced over her shoulder and found the area empty. "Never mind." She reached for her purse. "How much is a pass?"

"Just for today is four dollars."

Norah passed over some cash. "What's there to do here?"

The girl scanned Norah in her boots, jeans, and long-sleeved shirt. Standard attire for working with horses and girls, both of which Norah had done that day. "We have four basketball courts. Two are set up for pickleball tonight. There's a workout room upstairs, along with a weight room and an indoor walking track. All of our formal classes are in the mornin'." She gave Norah an apologetic smile. "We have a lap pool indoors, and it connects to our outdoor pool. That's down thatta way." She pointed in the general direction Sterling had gone.

"Locker rooms, and oh. Game rentals if you just want to come play board games." She beamed at Norah.

Though Norah's insides felt closer to liquefying, she managed to return the gesture. "I'll just check out the workout room."

"Sure thing." The girl sat back down and Norah hurried away from her. She felt like an imposter in the building, like everyone there would know she hadn't actually worked out in years. Like she carried a stink the die-hards could scent from miles away.

She didn't see Sterling upstairs, not that she expected him to change and start running after only five minutes. She found a bench overlooking one of the basketball courts and sat. On her left, she had a good view of the workout room, and in front of her, the occasional person walked or ran by on the track.

Sterling didn't surface.

She walked the track once, discovering that it overlooked all the basketball courts. He wasn't on any of them. The weight room boasted a dozen men with corded muscles, but none of them were Sterling.

He had to be in the pool. *Perfect,* Norah thought sarcastically as she went downstairs to figure out how to get to the pool. Everyone would notice a fully dressed woman walking through the pool area. Her step slowed as the smell of chlorine hit her nose. But her unhappiness urged her forward.

Do it, she told herself. *You promised not one more day would pass in this condition.*

The indoor area of the pool held only swimmers and two lifeguards. Outside, though, children and families created a cacophony of sound Norah wouldn't soon forget.

If she had to traipse through that to find Sterling.... Thoughts of leaning against his car until he came out filled her mind. She hadn't entirely decided against the idea when the door across from her opened. Two men came out—one of them Sterling.

He wore a swimming suit that looked more like biker shorts. The black material stretched to his knee and clung to his leg. His torso seemed bronzed, though he had to wear the same type of clothes to work that she did. He'd already hidden his hair beneath a swim cap, and now he laughed with the guy he was with. They moved down to two open lanes and adjusted their swim goggles over their eyes.

Norah admired Sterling's broad shoulders and strong arms, just like she admired his ability to show kindness. Sterling looked at the other man, and together they dove into the water. She watched them race through the water, disappearing under it when they drew close to the wall, flipping and heading back the way they came.

She stood transfixed. She'd never seen anyone in real life swim that way. Only on TV. During the Olympics. Familiar self-doubt clawed its way through her throat, almost choking her. She'd been to church twice since Sterling's frustrated words. She'd been praying every night. During the day. Whenever she saw him or thought about him—which meant she kept a prayer in her heart all the time.

She wished she felt beautiful the way some women did. She wished she knew how to do that, or that she could somehow turn it off and on like she did a faucet. She wished a great many things, but she'd been trying to be grateful for what she did have—and keep what she wanted.

Sterling.

The men reached the end of the lane, and Norah missed who won. But the way Sterling grinned, she suspected he had. Of course. The man excelled at everything he did. The pair continued swimming, the pace less feverish now. More controlled.

A whistle blew, and Norah jerked. "Can't stand there, ma'am."

She nodded at the lifeguard and hurried away from the end of the pool where Sterling swam. She took the only chair available on the border between the lap pool and the family swim area. Her stomach grumbled for food, but she stayed put. Finally, after about twenty minutes, the other man climbed out of the pool. He said something to Sterling, collected his towel, and left. Sterling swam.

And swam.

And swam.

Another twenty minutes passed before it even appeared he was slowing down. He paused at the wall where he'd started, and Norah sprang to her feet.

Now or never, she recited in time with her footsteps as

she rounded the pool to intersect him before he entered the locker room. He'd pulled himself from the water and was wiping his face with his towel when she arrived.

"Hi, Sterling," she said. "You swim?"

He stilled, his hand still cupping his chin with the towel. "Norah." He dropped his hands, giving her a full view of his body. "What are you doing here?"

She almost shrugged, as if to say, *Oh, you know. Here with the kids.*

"I followed you," she blurted out. "I've been following you for a couple of weeks."

His gaze remained steady and even, not even a hint as to what he was thinking. This was the man she'd expected to find in Denver but hadn't gotten. Then, he'd been readable, forgiving. Now, he seemed made of marble.

"I wanted to ask you if you'd go to the rodeo with me this weekend." She stepped back as another man exited the locker room. "It's the Fourth of July, and there's fireworks after. Me and the boys go every year."

The labored rise and fall of his chest was the only sign he was still alive.

"I already bought the ticket," she continued, the awkwardness between them growing into a tangible beast. "If you don't want it, I could ask—"

"I want it."

Happiness burst through Norah, unleashing the dam of words. "I'm so sorry, Sterling. I've been working on things, I swear. There's something wrong with me, and I'm trying to fix it." She moved closer to him, inhaled to draw some courage and bravery into her. She slipped her fingertips up his torso, noticing with delight the shiver her touch elicited in him.

"I love you," she said. "I believe you love me."

And at that moment, with all her heart and body and soul, she did.

———

One year later:

"It's so hot," Norah complained from his patio.

"Hey, you're the one who wanted a summer wedding," Sterling said from inside the kitchen, where the air conditioning kept everything cool. He lifted the lid on the pork roast Norah had put in the crockpot that morning and then returned to his task of staining a shelf he planned to put above the mantle in his bedroom.

If it were up to him, he would've married Norah *last* summer. But seeing as how she didn't really believe he loved her until July, and the one thing she wanted for her wedding was "no snow," he'd waited.

And waited.

And waited.

He was tired of waiting. Tired of living in his two-story house by himself. Tired of strapping his feet to a board and training and competing only to come in second, or third, or one time, seventh. Tired of only being able to kiss Norah and then drive away at night. He couldn't wait to be married.

Tomorrow, she'd come home with him.

Well, not technically. Tomorrow, after the wedding, they'd fly to LA and then board a cruise ship. But after that, he'd bring her home.

He'd moved in most of her stuff already. Even her luggage for their honeymoon sat near his front door.

"Last day at home," she murmured as she entered the house and slid the door closed behind her.

Sterling abandoned his home improvement project and swept Norah into his arms. "Norah, I'm your home now."

She tilted her head back and smiled at him in that sexy way she had. "Yes, you are."

He dipped his head to kiss her, the love passing between them almost more than Sterling could endure. "I love you, Norah."

"I know you do." She pressed herself closer to him, snaking her hands up his back. "Are you ready for tomorrow?"

What she really meant was, *We'll be okay, right? Even if Mama has a meltdown or your family gives me the evil eye?*

She'd met all his brothers, their wives, and their families in the past year. Everyone had been kind and accepting. Well, almost everyone. Emily still wouldn't look directly at her. And her mother was the definition of unpredictable.

"Tomorrow belongs to us," he assured her. "Just you and me. That's all that matters."

"You and me," she repeated.

"Me and you." Sterling kneaded her closer for another kiss, thinking he'd never get enough of the taste of her lips, never be able to spend enough time with her, never fathom how he'd gotten someone as beautiful and talented and caring as Norah to love him, whether he was a snowboarder, a policeman, or a horseback rider.

He broke the kiss, but stayed close to Norah. "Thank you for helping me see I had a life after the fall." He'd expressed similar gratitude to her—and the Lord—many times over the past year.

And every time, she said, "Guess God knew what He was doing after all," just like she did this time.

Sterling agreed, because he was finally in a place where he believed God loved him—both before *and* after the fall.

———

Read on for a sneak peek at **THE PREACHER'S DAUGHTER**, the next book in the Horseshoe Home Ranch Romance series.

Landon Edmunds woke to the sound of his phone vibrating against the decades-old dresser. For a moment, he wasn't sure where he was. The sun slanted through the window in the wrong spot.

He sat up, the familiar gray walls of his cabin coming into focus. "Not in Peach Valley anymore," he muttered as he reached for his cell. He'd taken a couple of weeks to get out of Montana before the summer planting started.

Sure, Jace needed him here all the time, as evidenced by the text on Landon's phone. *Need you at my place in fifteen minutes. Doable?*

Of course it was doable, whether Landon wanted to show his face around the ranch or not. He hadn't been able to escape his best friend's all-seeing eye, though he supposed he wouldn't want any less from the foreman at Horseshoe Home.

But Landon didn't want Jace's scrutiny any more than he

wanted his sister—and Jace's wife—to set him up with every able-bodied person with an X-chromosome. He was done with women, and his trip to Peach Valley had only solidified that decision.

Doable, he sent back to Jace and heaved himself out of bed. He wasn't supposed to work today either, but when Jace called, Landon answered. That road went both ways, as Landon had leaned on Jace's strength for most of this past year. And before that, Landon had helped Jace through a hard time after his fiancé abandoned him on his wedding day.

Grateful for good friends, Landon splashed water on his face and brushed his teeth. His phone chimed again, and he recoiled from a text from another cowboy about the first dance of the summer.

Landon used to lead the boys down the canyon to the valley dances. Cowboys were popular and he'd never had to scrounge for a partner. But he didn't want partners anymore. Not after Lauren had chosen him three years ago. Not after they dated for a year. Not after she decided another cowboy intrigued her more. Not after he found them kissing behind the barn.

They'd both left Montana now, thank goodness. For a while there, Landon had considered leaving the ranching business altogether. But he didn't have much else to do in his life. He loved ranching the same way he'd loved the rodeo. But he couldn't return to that career. The injury to his left leg prevented him from riding bulls ever again.

He had been considering leaving Horseshoe Home. He

and Jace had been looking at ranches all over the western United States, researching the cost to buy one, the time needed to move, to prepare the ranch, to get the best cowhands. Not that Jace was going to leave, but he'd done everything to support Landon.

Not going to the dance, Landon texted back to his friend. No reason. No excuse. Just not going. Hopefully Caleb wouldn't press the issue. Landon combed his hair and threw on a pair of jeans and a short-sleeved shirt in black-and-white plaid. He'd gotten a new hat from his friend in Peach Valley, and he mashed the black hat over his blond hair and headed out the door.

The first week of June in Montana sported an endless blue sky and temperatures Landon wished would stick for the whole year. He took a deep breath of the fresh mountain air, glad to be back in Big Sky Country.

His jaunt to Wyoming had been welcome, cleansing, but he'd realized he didn't want to move there. Sure, Jackson and Maya were wonderful and accommodating. It had been good to see his old friend from the rodeo, Jackson's brother, Blaze.

But Landon had realized on his two-week hiatus that he loved Montana. Had been born and raised here. But as he climbed the steps to Jace's front door, he still wasn't quite sure what he wanted.

He knocked at the same time he opened the door. "Mornin'," he called, closing the door behind him. Jace rose from an armchair at the same time Belle and a dark-haired woman twisted from their position on the couch to look at him.

Belle sprang to her feet, her face showing much more emotion than Jace's. Landon catalogued the fear, the nerves, and the hope in his sister's face before turning his attention to his best friend and boss.

"What's goin' on?" Landon glanced back to Belle, and then the second woman stood and faced him. A smile graced her familiar face, but Landon worked to recall who she was. Her beauty was obvious in the bones of her face, the depth of her dark eyes. She radiated an air that soothed Landon's soul, and his anxiety dropped a notch. Something about her called to him, made him want to get closer to her.

He worked hard to keep himself in place, looking to Jace and Belle for an explanation. He couldn't believe the attraction he felt; he'd sworn off dating and women. Completely. Totally. He'd been female-free for two years now.

But maybe this beautiful woman would break his—

"You remember Megan Palmer, don't you?" Belle wrung her hands, but put a smile on her face and in her voice.

All at once, recognition hit Landon full in the chest. "Megan Palmer." He settled his weight on his back foot and folded his arms. "Of course. The preacher's daughter."

She flinched, her smile folding for half a second before hitching back into place.

"She's helping out her dad for a while," Jace said. "Her father's retiring."

"That right?" Landon tore his eyes from the raven-haired beauty to flick his eyes to Jace for a moment. "That's great. What have you been up to?"

A shadow crossed her eyes, but when she said, "This and that," she sounded perfectly pleasant. Landon could read people, and he could tell she was hiding something. For some reason, he wanted to talk to her until he figured out what it was.

That's just because she's pretty, he told himself, strengthening his resolve not to let a familiar, gorgeous face persuade him from his bachelor life. Still, he had expected her to say she'd achieved something grand. She seemed like the type who would, the type Landon usually gravitated toward.

"She's just moved back from Wyoming," Belle said.

"Oh, I've just returned from a vacation in Wyoming."

"So Jace was telling me." Megan gave him that warm smile, and Landon basked in it. When he realized what was happening, he shut down his emotions.

"So what did you need, Jace?"

Jace settled back into the armchair, a sign that sent every alarm inside of Landon into red alert. He glanced at his sister, but she sat too, leaving his gaze to migrate to Megan. Still stunned by her beauty, and remembering her now from high school, he didn't quite understand when she said, "I'm afraid they got you over here so I could ask you for a favor."

———

Megan felt breathless. She'd prepared herself to be in the same room as her high school crush, Landon Edmunds. Or at least she'd thought she had. But facing him now, she knew she was ill-equipped to deal with his male magnetism, his stunning good looks, his wide shoulders. And her defenses against that sexy cowboy hat?

Nada.

She attempted to school her thoughts into something more godly, something that would represent a preacher's daughter. She hated the label that came with her name. She'd endured it growing up, and it really rubbed her the wrong way as an adult.

Of course, Landon didn't know that. Megan had never told her high school best friend, Belle, about her schoolgirl crush on her older brother. And he'd left for the rodeo circuit before she'd graduated from high school.

She'd always chalked up their separate lives as simply fate. But here she was, back in town, and Landon was nothing but available—if Belle was to be believed.

"Come on over and sit for a second," Jace said.

Landon obeyed him, and Megan fell heavily back to the couch beside Belle, her emotions spiraling up and then down. Had she really asked her best friend to set up a meeting with her brother? Like Megan was in junior high and couldn't use a phone to call the man herself.

Landon did not sit, but leaned against the kitchen counter and faced the living room. "Favor?" he asked, his attention on Megan singular.

She could barely breathe under the weight of it, and she

commanded herself to stop finding him so attractive. *Speak, Megan! Speak now.*

Belle elbowed her, and Megan cleared her throat. "That's right," she said, making her voice as smooth as she could. Thankfully, it flowed like honey. Dad had always said she had a soothing voice—something he'd used against her when he'd asked her to start teaching Bible Study classes.

"I'm helping my father get ready to retire, and I'm trying to get the church into shape before then." She exhaled, turning it into a laugh. "Well, before winter, really." Her eyes flitted all over the place, finally landing back on Landon. "That's where you come in."

He crossed his arms, making his biceps bigger and his presence fill the cabin. "Me?"

She swallowed and glanced at Jace, who nodded. "Yes, Jace says you've been looking for something different."

Though he made no sound, Megan could hear the internal growl Landon made as he swung his gaze to Jace. "He did, did he?" His voice sounded sharp, and cold, but Jace didn't so much as flinch.

"Don't look at me like that. You *have* been thinking about doing something different," he said. "This is carpentry work. You're the best cowhand when it comes to building repair."

"I have a job." One eyebrow rose. "At least I thought I did."

"You do," Jace said. "But I don't see why we can't loan you out to Miss Palmer for a few months."

"It's summer planting season," Landon said as if Megan and Belle weren't even in the room anymore. "You expressly told me I had to be back from Wyoming to start on Monday."

"And you're back a whole weekend early." Jace's steady gaze never left Landon's. The men seemed stuck in a battle of wills, and whoever looked away first would lose.

Jace sighed and glanced at Megan. "I can probably send out Ty. He's good with a hammer too."

"But Landon's the best," Belle piped up. Megan could feel her friend's nerves, and she smoothed her palms down her thighs.

"It's fine, guys," she said. "I can ask around town too." She stood and stepped over to Landon, her heart galloping, thundering, in her chest. She stretched up and kissed him on the cheek, startled at the spark of electricity that leapt from him to her. Or from her to him, she wasn't sure. "Good to see you again." She hastily stepped away and made for the front door.

She had to get out of there. *Get out. Get out quick.* She couldn't stand to be in Landon's presence for another second, though the twelve years since she'd seen him in person hadn't diminished her attraction to him at all.

She was surprised by that. Time should've been able to dim some of those feelings. Heck, her broken past with her recent ex should've been able to tame those emotions. But no, here she was, acting like a sixteen-year-old again, all infatuated with the gorgeous, strong cowboy.

She escaped and pressed her back to the closed front door. She finally managed to take a breath that wasn't filled with the scent of Landon's cologne, and reason infused her senses.

She did need help at the church. Her father hadn't been able to keep it up like he used to, not with his hip replacement five years ago. She'd hired Belle to do some interior design work, but she needed a handyman to really complete her vision for the project.

Voices behind the door filtered to her, and she hurried away, not wanting to eavesdrop on Landon as he questioned his family. Once in the safety of her car, Megan mentally recited the things she needed to accomplish before her father gave the congregation of Gold Valley to another pastor.

Fix up the building.

Repair the grounds.

Start community outreach programs.

Figure out how to teach the gospel.

Sure, she'd grown up listening to her dad preach. She loved going to church, and hearing the lectures, and reading the scriptures. But she hadn't gone to school, had never taken a theology class. Dad said the people wouldn't mind her lack of credentials just for Bible Study, but it bothered Megan.

She'd enrolled in several theology classes through the local college, and a couple online through the university in Missoula. With only seven months to get herself worthy to teach, the physical facilities were the least of her concerns.

She felt certain people would care if they found out her last boyfriend had stolen from her. They'd want their instructor to be smarter, know more, be more street-savvy, than that. She hadn't even told her father Eric's theft was the deciding factor in her return to Gold Valley.

Her dad had been asking her for a year to come home and help him teach, but she'd resisted. Eric lived and worked in Wyoming, and she'd been in love with him. As she turned back onto the highway and drove out of the canyon, she wondered if she still was.

Six months wasn't a very long time, and though he'd swindled dozens of people out of a lot of money—and taken thousands from Megan herself—she knew she needed more time to come to terms with how she felt about him, about herself, about everything, before she'd be ready to move forward.

"Maybe Landon can help you with that," she said. With her words came the fantasy of holding his hand, laughing with him, maybe even kissing him.

Annoyed with herself for even thinking such things about a man she no longer knew, Megan reached over and turned on the radio. Loud. She needed to use something to drive Landon from her mind.

Megan arrived at the church with a box of doughnuts and two mugs of coffee. She entered her father's office and found him seated behind the desk, bent over his notes. "Just how you like it, with sugar and cream," she said as she set the coffee next to him. "And I got you one of those apple fritters you like."

She put the box of baked goods next to him. He glanced up and smiled, though Megan saw the burdens he carried. That line of pain between his eyes from the hip that never stopped hurting. That edge of weariness in his eyes that had appeared when her mother had died four years ago. The pinch of his mouth because of the love he had for the people in Gold Valley. He prayed for them, thought of them often, served them when he could. The vein that pulsed in his neck with worry about someone else taking over the congregation.

"What are you studying this morning?" She reached for a long bar doughnut covered in whipped maple frosting.

"The Savior's teachings about charity."

"Deep." Megan bit into her doughnut, unsure of where the chapters on charity were located in the Bible. She had a ton of her own studying to do, but she couldn't seem to focus on it until late at night. Even then, Megan didn't have many scriptures memorized.

"A lifetime pursuit," he agreed. "Did you get a handyman?" His voice strayed a bit higher than she would've liked, his apology for the church needing a handyman.

"Not yet," she said. "But I will." She wanted it to be Landon, simply to be in his company. She may or may not have imagined confessing to him that she'd crushed on him for two years, that she'd followed his rodeo career online and on television for much longer than that.

She tucked her curly hair behind her ear and kept her thoughts silent. No one wanted to be told they'd been stalked, even through a screen. That wasn't romantic. As she polished off her doughnut, Megan was relieved Landon hadn't jumped at the chance to work for the church this summer. He didn't need to know what kind of pedestal she had him on, and she suddenly didn't want anyone to find out.

Yes, Megan had a lot to keep under wraps now that she was back in Gold Valley.

"Well, I'm gonna...." She hooked her thumb over her shoulder like that would convey to her father what she was going to go accomplish. He waved, his attention back on his scriptures, and she moved down the hall, noting the need for new paint on the walls, the crooked doorway on the men's restroom.

She definitely needed a handyman—and a boost of confidence that she could get the church and herself ready by January.

———

Landon had to practically fold himself in half to fit in the back of his sister's sedan. He hadn't seen or spoken to Jace or Belle since their "intervention" on Friday morning. After Megan had delicately removed herself from the conversation, he'd demanded to know what they'd been thinking.

His sister's words hadn't left his mind. *You can't be alone forever, Landon.*

When he'd challenged her and asked her why not, she'd looked to Jace for help. "Because that's not what people do," he'd said. "They get past hard things. They move on."

Landon had tried to tell them that he *was* past Lauren, but Jace—who'd been through a much more difficult experience when it came to women—hadn't believed him for a second. And he shouldn't. Landon knew he wasn't past Lauren. But he also knew that he'd spoken true when he'd told Belle and Jace that, "I'm just not interested in dating right now."

The miles passed as they continued toward the church. Landon had spent his Saturday wondering what it would take to get him interested in dating again. Flashes of

Megan's face, her calming influence, had plagued him all day.

"You think Megan will be there?" he asked as they passed the horseshoe-shaped falls where Jace and Belle had gotten engaged.

"'Course," Jace said.

His gut pinched, and he stared out the window without seeing much.

"You think any more about workin' for her?" Jace asked.

Landon checked his watch. "Twenty-four minutes," he said. "Which one of you wins the bet?"

"I do," Belle said at the same time Jace said, "There was no bet."

Landon laughed, the sound starting deep in his chest. While they frustrated him sometimes, Landon was grateful to have Belle and Jace in his life. They'd seen him at his worst and still wanted him around.

Jace pulled into the parking lot at the church. "All I'm sayin' is the church needs a handyman, and he could do it."

"I said you'd bring it up before church," Belle said. "I win."

"If I hadn't brought it up before church, you would've after. Then *I* would've won." He grinned at her, the love between them obvious and a tad infectious. Landon thought of Megan as he climbed out of the car, as Belle and Jace continued to bicker about who'd really won the bet. He followed them into the building and paused at the entrance into the chapel.

He kept his gaze forward though he wanted to scan for

dark, curly hair. His fingers balled into fists and his jaw ground together with the effort it took not to examine everyone who walked by. He spotted his parents and had a fleeting thought that he should just go sit by them, but Jace beckoned to him from a row in the middle of the chapel, and Landon stepped into the flow of people to take his place on the bench.

Landon didn't see Megan before the meeting started, and she didn't sit up front, and Landon's nerves felt raw and strained. As the closing prayer ended, relief poured through him. Relief he didn't quite understand. He thought he wanted to see her, maybe explain why he couldn't come work at the church.

But now that he didn't have to see her, talk to her, the relief combined with a sense of disappointment he didn't understand.

He stood and turned to leave, seizing when he found Megan only a foot from him. She startled too, her gaze flying up his chest to his face. "Landon," she said, his name almost a gasp.

He couldn't quite get his voice to work, so he swallowed and stepped back—right into Belle. "Sorry," he mumbled as he tried to figure out where to put himself that wouldn't be in someone's personal space.

Belle looped her arm through Landon's. "Hey, Megan." She released Landon and swept toward Megan for a hug. As Megan came closer to Landon, he caught a whiff of something floral.

She moved back and Landon found himself leaning

forward, still trying to identify that scent. He became very aware of Jace's gaze on the side of his face, and Landon put more distance between him and the very exotic smelling Megan.

He wasn't sure who said what, but he suddenly found himself alone, face-to-face with Megan. His boots made loud scuffing noises as he tried to find his center. The memory of her lips on his cheek—an innocent gesture from an old friend—now burned like a brand as he thought about her as a woman, not his little sister's best friend he used to know.

"Did you like the sermon?" she asked.

Landon blinked, his mind blank as to what the pastor had even said. "Uh, yeah. Sure. Great sermon." The lie seemed to echo around the near-empty chapel.

Megan cocked her head and grinned. "What did my father talk about?"

Landon rubbed the back of his neck. "I don't remember," he admitted with a soft chuckle. "I have a lot on my mind."

"Is working for the church one of them?" Megan asked, her eyes sparkling like dark, dangerous fireworks.

"You're a persistent little thing, aren't you?" Landon grinned at her.

"Let me take you on a tour of the building." She nodded toward the back of the chapel, a half smile on her full lips. "Do you have time?"

Landon's phone vibrated in his pocket. As if her question had reached Jace's ears, he'd texted to say they'd go up to the falls and he could text when he was ready to go.

With his mind whirling, and a ready excuse gone, he met Megan's eye. "I suppose I do."

"Great," she said. "Let's actually start right here in the chapel."

———

Read THE PREACHER'S DAUGHTER today! A billionaire cowboy, an unrequited crush, and a second chance start for these two best friends...

Scan the QR code below to get it!

Snowed in with the Cowboy (Book 2): Sterling Maughan, once a renowned snowboarder, is in self-imposed exile at his family cabin after a tragic accident stole his career. Lost and without purpose, solitude is his only companion until an unexpected visitor disrupts his isolation. **Can Norah trust Sterling enough to let him into her life and give their unexpected and forbidden love a chance?**

The Preacher's Daughter (Book 3): Landon Edmunds, a cowboy born and bred, has had his rodeo dreams realized and then dashed by a career-ending injury. Back in his hometown working at Horseshoe Home Ranch, he yearns for a new beginning with a ranch of his own. His sights are set on buying a horse ranch to train rodeo horses, but his plans take a detour when his high school best friend, Megan Palmer, steps back into his life. **Will they choose to follow their hearts, or will they let true love slip through their fingers again?**

Be sure to check out the spinoff series, the Brush Creek Cowboys romances after you read THE PREACHER'S DAUGHTER. Start with BRUSH CREEK COWBOY.

The Cowboy and the Nanny (Book 4): Twelve years ago, Owen Carr traded his roots and his sweetheart in Gold Valley for the bright lights of Nashville, where he found fame as a country music star. But when a tragic accident leaves him single-handedly raising his eight-year-old niece, Marie, he's forced to return home. Overwhelmed and out of his depth, Owen finds a lifeline in a most unexpected place. **As they mend bridges and explore the sparks that still sizzle between them, will they open their hearts to a second chance at love?**

Right Cowboy, Right Time (Book 5): Caleb Chamberlain, a fun-loving cowboy at Horseshoe Home Ranch, has spent the last five years wrestling with the ghosts of his past—a devastating breakup, alcoholism, and a near-fatal accident. Now, he's finally found solace in laughter and the rhythmic simplicity of ranch life. But a chance encounter with a familiar face threatens to upheave his newfound peace. **Can they navigate the shadows of the past to find their happily-ever-after?**

Second Chance Family (Book 6): Ty Barker has been living a carefree existence for the last thirty years. As friends around him found love and started families, Ty filled his time by giving horseback riding lessons and serving on a community service committee. But beneath the jovial surface, he's starting to feel the sting of loneliness. **He knows he wants River Lee in his life—but the question is, can he navigate the delicate steps needed to make her stay with him?**

The Christmas Cowboy Competition (Book 7): Archer Bailey has already had to yield one job to Emersyn "Emery" Enders. So when the opportunity of a cowhand job at Horseshoe Home Ranch presents itself, he keeps it to himself. Emery, whose temporary job is ending but whose responsibilities towards her physically disabled sister aren't, is left in the dark.

As the festive season unfolds, **will Emery and Archer navigate the complexities of the ranch, their close living arrangements, and their personal challenges to discover the love building between them? Or will their rivalry rob them of the greatest Christmas gift of all—true love?**

Love at First Cowboy (Book 8): Elliott Hawthorne, a career cowboy, has just witnessed his best friend and cabinmate forsake bachelorhood for matrimony. He'd be joyous if he weren't so green with envy. When a call about a family accident demands his presence, Elliott finds himself rushing from the ranch to his parents' house to see what's going on with his daddy, where he encounters the most stunning woman he's ever laid eyes on. **But as they encounter the complex dynamics of family responsibilities and personal desires, can their love-at-first-sight grow strong enough withstand the test of time?**

Brush Creek Cowboy (Book 1): Former rodeo champion and cowboy Walker Thompson trains horses at Brush Creek Horse Ranch, where he lives a simple life in his cabin with his ten-year-old son. A widower of six years, he's worked with Tess Wagner, a widow who came to Brush Creek to escape the turmoil of her life to give her seven-year-old son a slower pace of life. But Tess's breast cancer is back…

Walker will have to decide if he'd rather spend even a short time with Tess than not have her in his life at all. Tess wants to feel God's love and power, but can she discover and accept God's will in order to find her happy ending?

The Cowboy's Challenge (Book 2): Cowboy and professional roper Justin Jackman has found solitude at Brush Creek Horse Ranch, preferring his time with the animals he trains over dating. With two failed engagements in his past, he's not really interested in getting his heart stomped on again. But when flirty and fun Renee Martin picks him up at a church ice cream bar--on a bet, no less--he finds himself more than just a little interested. His Gen-X attitudes are attractive to her; her Millennial behaviors drive him nuts. Can Justin look past their differences and take a chance on another engagement?

A Cowboy Proposal (Book 3): Ted Caldwell has been a retired bronc rider for years, and he thought he was perfectly happy training horses to buck at Brush Creek Ranch. He was wrong. When he meets April Nox, who comes to the ranch to hide her pregnancy from all her friends back in Jackson Hole, Ted realizes he has a huge family-shaped hole in his life. April is embarrassed, heartbroken, and trying to find her extinguished faith. She's never ridden a horse and wants nothing to do with a cowboy ever again. Can Ted and April create a family of happiness and love from a tragedy?

A New Family for the Cowboy (Book 4): Blake Gibbons oversees all the agriculture at Brush Creek Horse Ranch, sometimes moonlighting as a general contractor. When he meets Erin Shields, new in town, at her aunt's bakery, he's instantly smitten. Erin moved to Brush Creek after a divorce that left her penniless, homeless, and a  single mother of three children under age eight. She's nowhere near ready to start dating again, but the longer Blake hangs around the bakery, the more she starts to like him. Can Blake and Erin find a way to blend their lifestyles and become a family?

The Cowboy and the Champion (Book 5): Emmett Graves has always had a positive outlook on life. He adores training horses to become barrel racing champions during the day and cuddling with his cat at night. Fresh off her professional rodeo retirement, Molly Brady comes to Brush Creek Horse Ranch as Emmett's protege. He's not thrilled, and she's allergic to cats. Oh, and she'd like to stay cowboy-free, thank you very much. But Emmett's about as cowboy as they come…. Can Emmett and Molly work together without falling in love?

Schooled by the Cowboy (Book 6): Grant Ford spends his days training cattle—when he's not camped out at the elementary school hoping to catch a glimpse of his ex-girlfriend. When principal Shannon Sharpe confronts him and asks him to stay away from the school, the spark between them is instant and hot. Shannon's

expecting a transfer very soon, but she also needs a summer outdoor coordinator—and Grant fits the bill. Just because he's handsome and everything Shannon's ever wanted in a cowboy husband means nothing. Will Grant and Shannon be able to survive the summer or will the Utah heat be too much for them to handle?

Second Chance Ranch: A Three Rivers Ranch Romance™ (Book 1): After his deployment, injured and discharged Major Squire Ackerman returns to Three Rivers Ranch, wanting to forgive Kelly for ignoring him a decade ago. He'd like to provide the stable life she needs, but with old wounds opening and a ranch on the brink of financial collapse, it will take patience and faith to make their second chance possible.

Third Time's the Charm: A Three Rivers Ranch Romance™ (Book 2): First Lieutenant Peter Marshall has a truckload of debt and no way to provide for a family, but Chelsea helps him see past all the obstacles, all the scars. With so many unknowns, can Pete and Chelsea develop the love, acceptance, and faith needed to find their happily ever after?

Fourth and Long: A Three Rivers Ranch Romance™ (Book 3): Commander Brett Murphy goes to Three Rivers Ranch to find some rest and relaxation with his Army buddies. Having his ex-wife show up with a seven-year-old she claims is his son is anything but the R&R he craves. Kate needs to make amends, and Brett needs to find forgiveness, but are they too late to find their happily ever after?

Fifth Generation Cowboy: A Three Rivers Ranch Romance™ (Book 4): Tom Lovell has watched his friends find their true happiness on Three Rivers Ranch, but everywhere he looks, he only sees friends. Rose Reyes has been bringing her daughter out to the ranch for equine therapy for months, but it doesn't seem to be working. Her challenges with Mari are just as frustrating as ever. Could Tom be exactly what Rose needs? Can he remove his friendship blinders and find love with someone who's been right in front of him all this time?

Sixth Street Love Affair: A Three Rivers Ranch Romance™ (Book 5): After losing his wife a few years back, Garth Ahlstrom thinks he's ready for a second chance at love. But Juliette Thompson has a secret that could destroy their budding relationship. Can they find the strength, patience, and faith to make things work?

The Seventh Sergeant: A Three Rivers Ranch Romance™ (Book 6): Life has finally started to settle down for Sergeant Reese Sanders after his devastating injury overseas. Discharged from the Army and now with a good job at Courage Reins, he's finally found happiness—until a horrific fall puts him right back where he was years ago: Injured and depressed. Carly Watters, Reese's new veteran care coordinator, dislikes small towns almost as much as she loathes cowboys. But she finds herself faced with both when she gets assigned to Reese's case. Do they have the humility and faith to make their relationship more than professional?

Eight Second Ride: A Three Rivers Ranch Romance™ (Book 7): Ethan Greene loves his work at Three Rivers Ranch, but he can't seem to find the right woman to settle down with. When sassy yet vulnerable Brynn Bowman shows up at the ranch to recruit him back to the rodeo circuit, he takes a different approach with the barrel racing champion. His patience and newfound faith pay off when a friendship--and more--starts with Brynn. But she wants out of the rodeo circuit right when Ethan wants to rejoin. Can they find the path God wants them to take and still stay together?

The Ninth Inning: A Three Rivers Ranch Romance™ (Book 8): The Christmas season has never felt like such a burden to boutique owner Andrea Larsen. But with Mama gone and the holidays upon her, Andy finds herself wishing she hadn't been so quick to judge her former boyfriend, cowboy Lawrence Collins. Well, Lawrence hasn't forgotten about Andy either, and he devises a plan to get her out to the ranch so they can reconnect. Do they have the faith and humility to patch things up and start a new relationship?

Ten Days in Town: A Three Rivers Ranch Romance™ (Book 9): Sandy Keller is tired of the dating scene in Three Rivers. Though she owns the pancake house, she's looking for a fresh start, which means an escape from the town where she grew up. When her older brother's best friend, Tad Jorgensen, comes to town for the holidays, it is a balm to his weary soul. A helicopter tour guide who experienced a near-death experience, he's looking to start over too--but in Three Rivers. Can Sandy and Tad navigate their troubles to find the path God wants them to take--and discover true love--in only ten days?

Eleven Year Reunion: A Three Rivers Ranch Romance™ (Book 10): Pastry chef extraordinaire, Grace Lewis has moved to Three Rivers to help Heidi Ackerman open a bakery in Three Rivers. Grace relishes the idea of starting over in a town where no one knows about her failed cupcakery. She doesn't expect to run into her old high school boyfriend, Jonathan Carver. A carpenter working at Three Rivers Ranch, Jon's in town against his will. But with Grace now on the scene, Jon's thinking life in Three Rivers is suddenly looking up. But with her focus on baking and his disdain for small towns, can they make their eleven year reunion stick?

The Twelfth Town: A Three Rivers Ranch Romance™ (Book 11): Newscaster Taryn Tucker has had enough of life on-screen. She's bounced from town to town before arriving in Three Rivers, completely alone and completely anonymous-- just the way she now likes it. She takes a job cleaning at Three Rivers Ranch, hoping for a chance to figure out who she is and where God wants her. When she meets happy-go-lucky cowhand Kenny Stockton, she doesn't expect sparks to fly. Kenny's always been "the best friend" for his female friends, but the pull between him and Taryn can't be denied. Will they have the courage and faith necessary to make their opposite worlds mesh?

Lucky Number Thirteen: A Three Rivers Ranch Romance™ (Book 12): Tanner Wolf, a rodeo champion ten times over, is excited to be riding in Three Rivers for the first time since he left his philandering ways and found religion. Seeing his old friends Ethan and Brynn is therapuetic--until a terrible accident lands him in the hospital. With his rodeo career over, Tanner thinks maybe he'll stay in town--and it's not just because his nurse, Summer Hamblin, is the prettiest woman he's ever met. But Summer's the queen of first dates, and as she looks for a way to make a relationship with the transient rodeo star work Summer's not sure she has the fortitude to go on a second date. Can they find love among the tragedy?

The Curse of February Fourteenth: A Three Rivers Ranch Romance™ (Book 13): Cal Hodgkins, cowboy veterinarian at Bowman's Breeds, isn't planning to meet anyone at the masked dance in small-town Three Rivers. He just wants to get his bachelor friends off his back and sit on the sidelines to drink his punch. But when he sees a woman dressed in gorgeous butterfly wings and cowgirl boots with blue stitching, he's smitten. Too bad she runs away from the dance before he can get her name, leaving only her boot behind...

Fifteen Minutes of Fame: A Three Rivers Ranch Romance™ (Book 14): Navy Richards is thirty-five years of tired—tired of dating the same men, working a demanding job, and getting her heart broken over and over again. Her aunt has always spoken highly of the matchmaker in Three Rivers, Texas, so she takes a six-month sabbatical from her high-stress job as a pediatric nurse, hops on a bus, and meets with the matchmaker. Then she meets Gavin Redd. He's handsome, he's hardworking, and he's a cowboy. But is he an Aquarius too? Navy's not making a move until she knows for sure…

Sixteen Steps to Fall in Love: A Three Rivers Ranch Romance™ (Book 15): A chance encounter at a dog park sheds new light on the tall, talented Boone that Nicole can't ignore. As they get to know each other better and start to dig into each other's past, Nicole is the one who wants to run. This time from her growing admiration and attachment to Boone. From her aging parents. From herself.

But Boone feels the attraction between them too, and he decides he's tired of running and ready to make Three Rivers his permanent home. **Can Boone and Nicole use their faith to overcome their differences and find a happily-ever-after together?**

The Sleigh on Seventeenth Street: A Three Rivers Ranch Romance™ (Book 16): A cowboy with skills as an electrician tries a relationship with a down-on-her luck plumber. Can Dylan and Camila make water and electricity play nicely together this Christmas season? Or will they get shocked as they try to make their relationship work?

The First Lady of Three Rivers Ranch: A Three Rivers Ranch Romance™ (Book 17): Heidi Duffin has been dreaming about opening her own bakery since she was thirteen years old. She scrimped and saved for years to afford baking and pastry school in San Francisco. And now she only has one year left before she's a certified pastry chef.

Frank Ackerman's father has recently retired, and he's taken over the largest cattle ranch in the Texas Panhandle. A horseman through and through, he's also nearing thirty-one and looking for someone to bring love and joy to a homestead that's been dominated by men for a decade. But when he convinces Heidi to come clean the cowboy cabins, she changes all that. But the siren's call of a bakery is still loud in Heidi's ears, even if she's also seeing a future with Frank. Can she rely on her faith in ways she's never had to before or will their relationship end when summer does?

Eighteen Bowties and Counting: A Three Rivers Ranch Romance™ (Book 18): He's her older brother's best friend and completely off-limits. She's got a way with horses...and a heart condition. Can Beau and Charlotte navigate close quarters to find their happily-ever-after?

Liz Isaacson writes inspirational romance, usually set in Texas, or Wyoming, or anywhere else horses and cowboys exist. She lives in Utah, where she writes full-time, takes her two dogs to the park everyday, and eats a lot of veggies while writing. Find her on her website at feelgoodfiction-books.com